"Tell me I'll be safe here, Jesse. I just need to know that for a little while I can let go of the fear."

As Jesse saw the haunting of her eyes, felt both the tragedy and the fear that emanated from her, he wished he could reassure her, promise her sanctuary, but Jesse had never been one to make false promises.

He knew nothing about her situation, knew nothing about what danger might find her here. He wouldn't lie, couldn't give her guarantees that didn't exist.

Something—an expression of need in her eyes—touched him, and he didn't like it. She was a job. Nothing more, nothing less. In two weeks she'd be gone, back to where she belonged.

Dear Reader,

As you have no doubt noticed, this year marks Silhouette Books' 20th anniversary, and for the next three months the spotlight shines on Intimate Moments, so we've packed our schedule with irresistible temptations.

First off, I'm proud to announce that this month marks the beginning of A YEAR OF LOVING DANGEROUSLY, a twelve-book continuity series written by eleven of your favorite authors. Sharon Sala, a bestselling, award-winning, absolutely incredible writer, launches things with *Mission: Irresistible,* and next year she will also write the final book in the continuity. Picture a top secret agency, headed by a man no one sees. Now picture a traitor infiltrating security, chased by a dozen (or more!) of the agency's best operatives. The trail crisscrosses the globe, and passion is a big part of the picture, until the final scene is played out and the final romance reaches its happy conclusion. Every book in A YEAR OF LOVING DANGEROUSLY features a self-contained romance, along with a piece of the ongoing puzzle, and enough excitement and suspense to fuel your imagination for the entire year. Don't miss a single monthly installment!

This month also features new books from top authors such as Beverly Barton, who continues THE PROTECTORS, and Marie Ferrarella, who revisits THE BABY OF THE MONTH CLUB. And in future months look for *New York Times* bestselling author Linda Howard, with *A Game of Chance* (yes, it's Chance Mackenzie's story at long last), and a special in-line two-in-one collection by Maggie Shayne and Marilyn Pappano, called *Who Do You Love?* All that and more of A YEAR OF LOVING DANGEROUSLY, as well as new books from the authors who've made Intimate Moments *the* place to come for a mix of excitement and romance no reader can resist. Enjoy!

Leslie J. Wainger
Executive Senior Editor

Please address questions and book requests to:
Silhouette Reader Service
U.S.: 3010 Walden Ave., P.O. Box 1325, Buffalo, NY 14269
Canadian: P.O. Box 609, Fort Erie, Ont. L2A 5X3

IMMINENT
DANGER

CARLA CASSIDY

Published by Silhouette Books

America's Publisher of Contemporary Romance

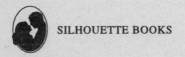 **SILHOUETTE BOOKS**

ISBN 0-373-27088-7

IMMINENT DANGER

Copyright © 2000 by Carla Bracale

Books by Carla Cassidy

CARLA CASSIDY

is an award-winning author who has written over thirty-five books for Silhouette. In 1995, she won Best Silhouette Romance from *Romantic Times Magazine* for *Anything for Danny*. In 1998, she also won a Career Achievement Award for Best Innovative Series from *Romantic Times Magazine*.

Carla believes the only thing better than curling up with a good book to read is sitting down at the computer with a good story to write. She's looking forward to writing many more books and bringing hours of pleasure to readers.

IT'S OUR 20th ANNIVERSARY!
We'll be celebrating all year,
Continuing with these fabulous titles,
On sale in July 2000.

Intimate Moments

#1015 Egan Cassidy's Kid
Beverly Barton

#1016 Mission: Irresistible
Sharon Sala

#1017 The Once and Future Father
Marie Ferrarella

#1018 Imminent Danger
Carla Cassidy

MMM **#1019 The Detective's Undoing**
Jill Shalvis

#1020 Who's Been Sleeping in Her Bed?
Pamela Dalton

Special Edition

#1333 The Pint-Sized Secret
Sherryl Woods

#1334 Man of Passion
Lindsay McKenna
50th book

#1335 Whose Baby Is This?
Patricia Thayer

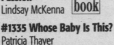
#1336 Married to a Stranger
Allison Leigh

#1337 Doctor and the Debutante
Pat Warren

#1338 Maternal Instincts
Beth Henderson

Desire

#1303 Bachelor Doctor
Barbara Boswell

#1304 Midnight Fantasy
Ann Major

#1305 Wife for Hire
Amy J. Fetzer

TEXAS GROOMS **#1306 Ride a Wild Heart**
Peggy Moreland

#1307 Blood Brothers
Anne McAllister & Lucy Gordon

#1308 Cowboy for Keeps
Kristi Gold

Romance

AN OLDER MAN **#1456 Falling for Grace**
Stella Bagwell

#1457 The Borrowed Groom
Judy Christenberry

#1458 Denim & Diamond
Moyra Tarling

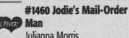
#1459 The Monarch's Son
Valerie Parv

#1460 Jodie's Mail-Order Man
Julianna Morris

#1461 Lassoed!
Martha Shields

Chapter 1

They hadn't told him she was blind.

Jesse Wilder stared out his living room window, watching the beige sedan that had pulled up at the curb. The driver helped a woman from the car then handed her the traditional white-tipped cane for the blind.

Jesse frowned, his mind racing with how the woman's sight limitations might complicate things. Already everything was complicated enough.

As the couple drew closer, Jesse studied them intently. He knew the man was Kent Keller, the U.S. Marshal who, along with Bob Sanford, had set up this whole thing. He didn't yet know the woman's name, and in any case would probably never be privy to her real name.

In Jesse's eight years of working in law enforcement, the last four as Sheriff of Mustang, Montana, he'd never been involved in anything like this. He wouldn't be now if Bob Sanford hadn't asked for his help.

He narrowed his eyes, studying the woman, her cane awkwardly tapping the sidewalk in front of her.

It was difficult to discern much about her features. Oversize glasses and dark bangs obscured the top portion of her face, and the late-summer breeze blew a strand of her long dark hair across her cheek, further cloaking her features.

Protective custody for a week or two. Jesse's responsibility was to keep this woman out of harm's way.

He moved away from the window as the couple approached the house. A moment later a knock sounded. Drawing a deep breath, Jesse answered the door.

"Sheriff Wilder?" The tall, gray-haired man had eyes like flint and his face looked as if it had never known the softness of a smile.

"Yes, sir," Jesse replied, fighting the automatic impulse to salute the stern man.

"I'm Marshal Keller."

He shook Keller's hand hard and met his icy gaze unflinchingly.

Jesse stepped aside to allow them entry into his home. "Please, come in."

As he closed the front door, Keller helped the young woman to the sofa. She sank down on the cushion and Keller sat beside her. Jesse sat in a chair facing them, waiting patiently, knowing Keller would tell him only what he needed to know.

"Sheriff Wilder, this is..."

"Cecilia, Cecilia Webster." Her voice was low and soft, and he knew instantly that the name was a lie. It fell uneasily from her lips, as if she were testing the sound of it.

"Nice to meet you both. I assume you had no trouble finding the place." Jesse said.

"No problems," Keller replied, offering no information on how long they'd been driving or how far they'd come.

"Have you ever been to Montana before, Ms. Webster?" Jesse asked.

"No. It's never been particularly high on my list of places I wanted to go."

"But now we're here, and that's that," Keller said flatly.

"Would you like something to drink? Something to eat, perhaps?" Jesse offered.

"No, thanks," Keller replied.

An uncomfortable silence fell among them. Keller looked at Jesse and nodded toward the door. "Why don't you walk me out? You can get Ms. Webster's things from the car. I need to get back on the road."

Keller stood. "Cecilia, I'll be in touch."

She nodded, appearing to grow smaller as she wrapped her arms around herself and sank deeper into the sofa cushions.

Jesse followed Keller outside. The older man said nothing until they reached the car. "We thought the investigation she's involved with would only take a couple of weeks, but it's taking longer. For the last month we've had her in dozens of motel rooms. But mentally she hasn't been handling it real well, so we decided she needed something more permanent.'' He opened the trunk and withdrew a large suitcase and a smaller, overnight bag.

"Why not the Witness Protection Program?" Jesse asked.

"Because the people she will be testifying against could possibly have access to information from the Witness Protection Program. We couldn't take the risk. We decided to go outside the system to try to find her a safe haven."

Jesse was definitely intrigued. "But why me?" It was a question that had plagued him since the initial phone call from Sanford.

For the first time a ghost of a smile lifted the corners of Keller's mouth. "Mustang, Montana, isn't exactly a well-known metropolis. I don't know of anyone who even knows Mustang exists."

"I wouldn't say that to the citizens that call Mustang home," Jesse said dryly.

Keller closed the trunk, then looked at Jesse once again. "We chose you for several reasons. The town is small, your record is excellent and you have no family."

Jesse almost smiled. Keller obviously didn't know about small-town living where everyone considered everyone else family of sorts.

"We also know you have no close personal relationships, no wife, no girlfriend."

The smile that almost made it to Jesse's lips instantly dissipated as he wondered how deeply they'd delved into his private life.

"Besides," Keller continued, "Sanford said you owed him and you wouldn't tell us no."

Bob Sanford had been his mentor when Jesse had gone to the police academy. Without Bob's personal interest and patience, Jesse would not have made it through the grueling training.

"So, is there anything specific I need to know?" Jesse asked.

"Just go about your business as usual. As much as possible, try not to break from your normal routine. Tell anyone who asks that she's your girlfriend, come to stay for a brief visit. Basically your job is that of glorified baby-sitter." Keller walked around to the driver's door and opened it. "We aren't expecting any problems. There are only three of us who know her actual location. Still, you shouldn't forget that she is at the center of an investigation that puts her life at risk.

"She's a material witness that's vital to the investigation. Trust nobody, and make sure she doesn't, either." Keller slid behind the wheel and started the engine. "I'm sure everything will be fine. She's a long way from the bad guys here."

Dozens of questions whirled in Jesse's mind. "How do I get in touch with you if I need to?"

"You don't." Keller slammed the car door and pulled away from the curb.

Jesse watched the car until it disappeared from his sight, then he turned and eyed the neat, three-bedroom ranch-style house he called home. For the next week or two he would share his home with a blind material witness whose life was in danger. How could a blind woman be a witness to anything?

Questions spun through his mind, but Jesse knew he could expect no answers. Keller had told him what he absolutely needed to know—nothing more, nothing less.

When he walked inside, Cecilia was sitting exactly where they had left her, the dark glasses still perched over her eyes.

He wondered about her blindness. How long had she been blind? Had she been blind since birth or had she enjoyed the wonder of sight only to lose it through some tragedy?

Some place deep inside him, a grievous memory stirred to the surface, but he mentally shoved it away as he had done countless times in the past.

''Sheriff Wilder?'' There was a slight panic in her voice.

''Yes, it's me,'' he answered hurriedly and set down the two suitcases. ''But you'd better call me Jesse. According to Keller, I'm supposed to tell everyone that you're my girlfriend.''

''Lucky you,'' she said, an underlying bitterness scoring her words.

Jesse shifted from one foot to the other, unsure what to do next. ''Can I get you something to drink? Are you hungry?'' He'd asked before, but she hadn't replied.

''No, I'm fine for now.'' She lay the cane next

to her and entwined her fingers in her lap. "If I'm going to play the part of your girlfriend, then I guess we should come up with some background story."

Jesse once again sat in the chair facing her. He'd never before realized how he depended on seeing a person's eyes to assess their character. He found the dark glasses rather disconcerting.

"Since you've never been to Mustang before, we would have to have met someplace else." He frowned thoughtfully. "A couple months ago I took a week's vacation and went camping. We could tell people I met you then."

She frowned, her nose wrinkling. "I don't know anything about camping. Besides, who would believe I was out in the wilderness setting up a tent?"

She had a point. "Well, then maybe we could have met in a café as I was driving home," he offered.

"And what was I doing there? Serving coffee? Short-order cook?"

Unexpected irritation surged in Jesse. "Lady, you've got to help me out here," he said.

Her cheeks pinkened and she tugged off the glasses, exposing beautiful large green eyes fringed with dark, thick lashes. "I apologize. Perhaps I'm more tired than I realized. Would it be possible to show me to my room and we can discuss the details of everything a little bit later?"

Jesse instantly regretted snapping at her. Without the glasses, he could see bruiselike dark circles beneath her eyes. That, coupled with her pale complexion, gave her the appearance of sheer exhaustion. "Of course. Let me get your bags into the room, then I'll come back for you."

"I appreciate it."

For the first time since buying the house, Jesse was grateful the guest bedroom was stark. A double bed, a chest of drawers and a nightstand were the only furniture. At least it wouldn't be too much of a challenge for a blind person to maneuver.

He set the suitcases in the bottom of the empty closet, then returned to the living room. She was standing, cane in one hand, the sunglasses propped on the top of her head.

"Here we go," he said, self-consciously taking her by the elbow. "There's a long hallway and your room is the second on the left. The bathroom is the first door on the left."

She held herself stiffly, as if she were unaccustomed to another's touch. Jesse could feel the tension that rippled from her, waves of nervous anxiety almost visible in its strength.

And why shouldn't she be tense? he asked himself. Under the best of circumstances, it would be difficult to be blind. She had the added burden of knowing she was in danger, and she'd just been dropped off at a stranger's house in an unfamiliar town.

"The bed is straight ahead, the chest of drawers to the left, the closet on the right," Jesse explained as they turned into the bedroom doorway. "There's a nightstand on the left of the bed, and I put your suitcases in the closet." He hesitated a moment, unsure about her needs. "Do you want me to help you unpack?"

"No, thanks. I'm sure I can manage just fine." Her voice was cool, as if he'd irritated her with his question. She stepped away from him, so he was no longer touching her.

"Then I'll just leave you to rest," he said. "Do you want the door open or closed?"

"Closed."

Jesse shut the door, then returned to the living room. Moving to the window, he stared outside, his thoughts now focused on his new houseguest.

Cecilia was blind, beautiful and prickly as a cactus. Of course, not knowing exactly what had happened in her life, what she found herself involved in, it was difficult for him to cast stones because of her irritable mood.

Jesse rubbed his hands down the sides of his jeans, realizing his palms were damp with nervous sweat. A blind woman in his care. Was this somebody's idea of retribution? Reparation for the unresolved trauma in his life?

Again that distant memory knocked in his brain. For an instant, he saw everything as it had been on that night so long ago. The headlights of his car shining on the black glaze of the road...the pull of the steering wheel as the car went out of control...the thick, twisted tree that loomed closer...closer until... Jesse gasped and forcefully shoved the memories away. He turned from the window.

One week. Two at the most, and then she'd be

gone from his life. Surely for two weeks he could take care of her, keep her safe and not think about the past, about the man whose life he'd destroyed on a wintry slick road almost thirteen years ago.

Seven steps from the doorway to the edge of the bed. Five steps from the bed to the chest of drawers and four from the bed to the closet. Her entire world had become comprised of steps.

She sank onto the edge of the bed. "My name is Allison Welch," she whispered to herself. "Allison Welch. Allison Welch."

Like a mantra, she repeated it over and over again, afraid that one of these days Allison Welch would somehow cease to exist altogether.

Allison Welch had the world by the tail. She was an up-and-coming interior designer, and her shop, Comforts Of Home, was gaining more and more popularity in Chicago.

She had a fantastic apartment overlooking Lake Michigan, a full social life and a close relationship with her sister and brother-in-law.

A sob rose and she slapped a hand across her mouth to contain it. She wouldn't think about Alicia and John and that night. If she let those horrendous visions replay, she'd lose her mind.

Unpack. Deal with the here and now. If she thought of the past, grief would overwhelm her. If she tried to anticipate the future, fear and despair would engulf her.

Four steps to the closet and she found her suit-cases on the floor. She grabbed the big one and carried it back to the bed, where she clicked it open and began to unpack. There weren't a lot of clothes inside, and everything was already on a hanger.

They all had been bought by a female officer when Allison had been released from the hospital a month ago. A dress, two pairs of jeans, a pair of dress slacks, two T-shirts, three sweatshirts and two silk blouses, all in shades of blue so she could dress herself and not worry about clashing colors.

The smaller suitcase held toiletries, underclothes and her nightgown and robe. She finished unpacking, then once again sat on the edge of the bed. At least it would be nice to be in the same place for more than three days.

The last month was a blur of motel and hotel rooms. Her knees and shins were bruised by the fact that they hadn't been in any one room long enough for her to learn navigating the furniture. Just as she'd figured out how to walk in the room without bumping into something, they'd move to a new place.

She thought of her host. Jesse Wilder. All she knew about him was that he was sheriff of Mustang, Montana.

Well, that wasn't exactly true. She also knew he had a deep voice as soothing as a velvet wrap on a wintry night. As he'd led her into the bedroom, she'd gotten the impression that he was tall, and smelled of the pleasant combination of soap and spice cologne.

She had no idea how old he was, what he looked like or if she could trust him. Although she assumed

Kent Keller and Bob Sanford wouldn't have placed her in his care if he couldn't be trusted.

She frowned at thoughts of the two men who'd been in charge of her life for the past month. Blind, and reeling from what she'd experienced, it had taken a considerable amount of reassurance from Bob Sanford before she'd tell him anything about what she'd seen from the closet.

Once Sanford had been assured by her doctor that physically she was ready to be released, she'd been transferred to Keller's care and had begun the motel room jumping that had eventually brought her here.

She pulled her glasses off the top of her head and placed them on the nightstand, then stretched out across the bed. The spread smelled of sunshine and fabric softener.

The moment she'd walked in, she'd noticed the entire house had the odor of lemon wax and cleanser. Sheriff Wilder had obviously cleaned for her arrival.

Tears pressed hot and heavy at her eyes as she thought of all she'd lost. Everything. She'd lost everything. She'd gladly accept the blindness for the rest of her life if in return she could give John and Alicia back their lives.

She squeezed her eyes tightly closed, knowing that was impossible. John and Alicia were gone forever. Murdered in their home. No sacrifice on Allison's part, no bargaining with the devil or with God would bring them back. The best she could hope for was to bring down the men responsible for their deaths.

As she had done for the past four weeks, she consciously willed away her tears, refusing to give in to grief. Retribution. That had become her reason for being, the sum total of her existence. The guilty had to be punished.

This was the goal that kept her from sinking into the utter depths of despair, from giving up all pretense of living.

She would survive whatever fate threw her way…as long as in the end, the people responsible for John and Alicia's deaths paid.

She rolled over on her side, staring blankly at the window, where she could feel the sun warming the spread, splashing her face.

She was supposed to be Cecilia Webster now, a twenty-six-year-old blind woman from Cleveland, Ohio.

It was an identity provided for her protection, but she hadn't felt safe one moment in the past four weeks.

A couple more weeks. That's what Keller had promised her. In a couple more weeks the investigation should be over and the killers would be behind bars. Then she could return to her life…at least the shattered pieces that were left.

She closed her eyes, hoping, praying for the sweet release that sleep could bring, hoping, praying that the nightmares that so often plagued her sleep remained at bay.

*   *   *

Jesse looked at his watch for the third time in twenty minutes. His houseguest had been in the bedroom for nearly three hours and he hadn't heard a peep.

While she'd slept, he'd made dinner, deciding on hamburgers and chips. Not exactly a gourmet welcome meal, but simple and easy to eat.

He checked his watch yet again. After six. He wondered if perhaps he should wake her, but was reluctant to intrude on her sleep if that's what she needed. He supposed she'd get up when she was hungry, and in the meantime all he could do was wait.

He walked into the kitchen, grabbed a cold soda from the refrigerator and popped the top. He took a long swallow, then moved to the window to stare outside.

He'd called the sheriff's office earlier to let Vic Taylor, one of his deputies know he needed to take a day or two off. Even though Keller had told him to keep a normal routine, he couldn't very well leave a blind woman to her own devices in strange surroundings.

He'd begun to perpetuate the cover story, telling Vic that a friend had stopped by for a surprise visit.

There had been no new breaks on the Casanova case, nothing else pressing that couldn't wait a day or two. Vic had assured him that the four deputies could handle whatever arose and Jesse had hung up, knowing the people who worked for him were good, competent and fair lawmen.

He took another sip of his soda and moved away

from the window with another glance at his watch. A scream ripped through the silence of the house.

For an instant, Jesse froze. The scream had come from the guest room. Adrenaline pumped through him. He slammed his drink down and grabbed his gun from the holster hanging on a hook near the back door. He flipped off the safety and advanced slowly, cautiously down the hallway.

Had somebody managed to track her here? Was somebody in the bedroom with her now? Damn Keller for not telling him more. Damn Keller for not warning him she might be in imminent danger.

He reached the closed bedroom door and paused, listening for a sound, any sound that might indicate what was happening on the other side of the hollow wood. Nothing. Not a sound. Not a single noise.

Was she already dead? Would he open the door to find her lifeless body draped across the bed? If somebody had entered through the window, she would have never seen him coming. She wouldn't have known she wasn't alone in the room until hands had closed around her throat, or a blade had touched the flesh of her neck.

Jesse grabbed the doorknob and turned it slowly, soundlessly. Although emotion demanded he hurry—fling open the door and burst inside—training and instinct warned him to go slow, to face the unknown with caution. He eased the door open and stepped inside, the gun leveled in front of him.

Nothing.

The room appeared empty. The bedspread was wrinkled and a depression marked the center of one of the pillows. The window was closed, the curtains neatly in place. Nothing looked out of the ordinary, except Cecilia Webster was no place in sight.

A renewed burst of adrenaline flooded him as he heard a thump come from the closet. The closet door was half-open, but the waning light of dusk threw deep shadows that obscured the interior of the small space.

Jesse advanced, his gun once again leading the way. With one hand, he eased the closet door fully open. She was there.

He lowered his gun and muttered a soft curse beneath his breath. As he gazed at her, curled up in the corner, her eyes squeezed tightly shut and her cheeks stained with tears, he wondered what in the hell she'd been through, and what in the hell he'd gotten himself into!

Chapter 2

She could see through the wooden slats of the closet door, saw the two men burst into the house with their guns drawn.

"Hey. Hey…!" John exclaimed. "What's wrong? What's going on?"

Allison watched in horror as her sister and brother-in-law backed away from the men, stood just in front of where she hid in the closet.

"Don't do anything stu—" John's voice was lost in the eruption of gunfire.

Gunshots resounded in the air. A total of six. Miniexplosions not loud enough to penetrate the walls of the house, not loud enough to beckon help. But loud enough, strong enough for the bullets to kill John and Alicia.

John fell forward, crashing to the floor like a

huge oak felled by a lumberjack's ax. Alicia flew backward and smashed into the closet door. A bullet slammed into the wall just above Allison's head. Blood splattered through the slats, a fine spray on her face, her chest.

Shoving a hand against her mouth, Allison tried to still a scream of disbelieving terror. No! Oh, God…no! This couldn't be happening. Her mind raced frantically to make sense of the scene unfolding in front of her.

She fought the impulse to run to her sister, to try to help her. Someplace in her terror-filled mind, the instinct of survival kept her rooted in her hiding place.

Quiet. She had to stay quiet. If they found her, they'd kill her, too. She had to stay alive. She had to stay alive so she could tell somebody what happened here….

"Cecilia."

The voice came from some distant place, but it had nothing to do with her. She squeezed her eyes tightly shut and shoved her hand harder against her mouth.

Blood. There was too much blood. Alicia was dead—murdered, her blood on Allison's face. Dear God, all that blood. Why had this happened? Why? Why?

"Cecilia!" The deep male voice called again, this time more forcefully.

She shrank deeper into the closet, pressing her back into the corner in an attempt to escape.

A stinging slap across one of her cheeks jarred

her from her nightmare landscape to the present. In an instant, she realized she was a long way from John and Alicia's home. She was in Montana. Mustang, Montana.

"Sheriff Wilder?" she whispered hesitantly.

"Jesse," he corrected her. "I'm right here." His hand closed around one of hers. His hand was large and warm, and offered comfort despite its unfamiliar feel.

Her other hand reached up, hit clothes hanging above her. "I'm in the closet, aren't I?" Weary discouragement weighed heavy on her shoulders.

"Yeah." His hand tightened around hers. "Why don't we get you out of here?"

She'd had the nightmare again. No, not a nightmare, but rather a tormenting replay of the horror she'd endured. And, as always, she'd sought the safety of the nearest closet.

When would this end? Would her life—would *she* ever be normal again?

Embarrassment battled with overwhelming despair as he guided her out of the small confines and into the bedroom. "How did you know I was in there?" she asked. With a tinge of reluctance, she pulled her hand from his.

"You screamed."

"I'm sorry. I was asleep. It was a nightmare." She crossed her arms in front of her and hugged her shoulders with her hands. "I guess Keller didn't warn you about my nightmares."

"Keller didn't tell me much about anything," he said dryly. "Are you all right?"

She released a sigh. "Embarrassed. Mortified, but yes, I'm all right."

"No need to be embarrassed," Jesse said in an obvious attempt to comfort. "Everyone has nightmares at one time or another."

She said nothing, but she wanted to say that not everyone had nightmares that drove them into the deepest recess of a closet.

"If you're hungry, I've got some dinner ready in the kitchen," he said.

Dinner. The normalcy of it further comforted her. "That sounds good. I'd just like to freshen up a bit."

"Sure. I'll just wait in the living room for you, then take you to the kitchen." She nodded. She hated this dependency, she thought as Jesse left her alone at the bathroom door. A moment later she splashed water over her face and stared at the place where she knew a mirror probably hung over the sink.

Staring with all the concentration she could attain, she tried to force herself to see. A glimmer of light. A pale strand of illumination.

She desperately wanted to see something...anything. But the blackness that had become her world remained impenetrable.

It was as if she'd swallowed whole the darkness of night, and the tenebrous shades of black not only resided in her, but had become the sum being of her.

Odd, that even in complete darkness, while

asleep and in the throes of a nightmare and in a strange house, she had found the closet.

Had she fumbled her way to the enclosure that comforted her? Or had her sight momentarily returned while she'd dreamed, allowing her to find the closet where she could hide and feel safe?

Turning away from the sink, she felt around until her hands touched the terry cloth of a towel. She dried her face and hands, then left the bathroom. Carefully maneuvering out the door and down the hallway, she headed toward the living room. She stifled a gasp as a hand touched her elbow.

"Sorry, I didn't mean to startle you," Jesse said.

"It's all right. It's just disconcerting to be touched when you can't see who is doing the touching." She relaxed and allowed him to guide her through the living room. She knew they'd entered the kitchen when the carpet beneath her feet turned into tile.

"I hope you like hamburgers," Jesse said as he led her to a chair at the table.

"Hamburgers are fine," she assured him. She touched the edge of her plate, the handle of a fork to orient herself.

"Mustard or ketchup?" Jesse asked.

"A little mustard, please." She heard the squirt of a bottle, then sensed him placing the burger on her plate. "Thank you."

"Chips?" he offered.

"Sure," she agreed, just wanting to get the meal over and done with. Eating was one of the many things that had become sheer torture since she'd lost her sight. Finger food had become her friend.

Within minutes they were eating, the meal accompanied by the strained silence of strangers who weren't quite sure what to say to each other.

"So, tell me about Mustang, Montana," she said in an effort to break the uncomfortable silence.

"There isn't a lot to tell. Small town, slow pace, good people. It's a great place to grow up and a great place to grow old."

"You love it here," she observed. She'd heard the warmth in his voice as he spoke of the town.

"I do," he agreed. "Mustang is a small town with a big heart. I left for four years to go to college, then went on to the police academy, but my heart never really ever left."

"That's nice," she said. "Do you have family here?"

The moment the question left her lips, the despair of her loss echoed within her heart.

Never again would she be able to share with her sister the laughter or the tears that life so often contained. Never again would she know the comfort of a sisterly hug.

"No, no family. My father died three years ago in a car accident and my mother passed away seven months later. The doctors said it was heart failure, but I'll always believe it was a broken heart."

He cleared his throat, as if embarrassed by the personal disclosure. "Actually, even though I have no blood family here, everyone in Mustang acts like they're family. Everyone knows everyone else's business, and if you have a problem of any kind, somebody is always ready with advice.''

"If everyone knows everyone else's business, then I guess it would be smart for us to know our business,'' she said.

"You're talking about our cover story.''

She nodded and chewed a chip thoughtfully. "I really hate to tell people we met while camping because I know absolutely nothing about it.''

"You've really never been on a camp out? Didn't you ever sleep in the backyard with friends or go to Girl Scout camp?''

She heard the incredulity in his voice. "No outdoor sleepovers, no Girl Scouts. The closest I've ever come to camping out was when my sister and I made a tent in our bedroom and pretended we were wilderness guides.''

The memory brought with it a glow of happiness as she remembered that night. She and Alicia had fashioned a tent from the top of their dresser to the top of their bed. They'd spent hours making shadow animals on the ceiling with the aid of a flashlight.

They'd eaten an entire package of cookies while making up scary stories to entertain each other. Their mother had grounded them the next morning when she'd seen the mess they had made, but the night's adventure had been worth the punishment.

The warmth of the memory battled with the coldness of loss, creating a whirlwind of grief to whip through her.

"Cecilia?" Jesse pulled her from the memory.

"We can tell everyone we met camping," she

said, suddenly changing her mind. "We can tell them I was camping with my sister and you were at the site next to ours. I don't think anyone will really ask me about the actual camping experience, do you?"

"I sincerely doubt it." She heard the crunch as he ate a potato chip, then he continued. "And we'll tell everyone that since that time we've been burning up the phone lines."

She nodded. "Then it's official. You now have a girlfriend." She finished the last bite of her hamburger, then gazed across to where she knew he sat. "Will people think it odd that you fell in love with a blind woman?"

"People will find it odd that I'm in love with anyone."

Again she heard a smile in his voice. "Why is that?" she asked curiously.

"I've been the elusive bachelor of Mustang for a long time now. Mothers try to set me up with their daughters, aunts corner me in stores and tell me about the charms of their nieces."

"You must be very good-looking," she observed.

The smile she'd heard in his voice turned into full-blown laughter. He had a wonderful laugh. Deep and resonant, it brought with it a wealth of warmth that fluttered inside her, momentarily banishing the frozen tears that had encased her heart.

"No, not particularly good-looking," he replied. "Just one of the few young, available bachelors in town. Besides, you know what they say about women and men in uniform.''

Men in uniform. Suddenly her body went cold. John and Alicia had worn the blue uniforms of the Templeton Police Department.

They had loved working law enforcement in the small Chicago suburb. Uniforms with badges. Symbols of safety. And yet the thought of those badges and dark blue outfits evoked dreadful disquiet. Forcefully she shoved away thoughts of her last family.

Instead she focused on the man across from her, the man she could smell, could sense, but couldn't see. "How old are you?" she asked.

"Didn't your mother ever tell you it wasn't polite to ask somebody their age?" There was a soft, teasing lilt to his tone.

"My mother taught me that if you want to know something, ask."

"Smart woman, your mother. I'm almost thirty."

"Why haven't you married and started a family? I thought people in small towns married young."

"Relationships have always seemed too complicated and difficult to maintain. I love my job, I like my home. That's always been enough for me."

She smiled. "No wonder you're considered a catch. There's nothing like the challenge of a confirmed bachelor to whet the appetite of single women."

"Speaking of appetites, would you like another hamburger?"

"No, thanks. I'm fine." She heard his chair scoot

back and knew he'd gotten up from the table. "I'm sorry I can't help with the cleanup. Dishes that feel clean don't always look clean."

"Don't worry about it."

"It's not real." The words fell from her mouth without any warning.

"Excuse me?"

"My blindness. It's not real."

There was a long moment of silence. "What do you mean? Are you faking your blindness?" She heard the bewilderment in his voice.

"No, the blindness is real, but there's no physical reason for it. It's psychosomatic. Hysterical blindness is what the doctors call it." She couldn't help the anger that sharpened her tone.

She was sorry she'd brought it up. The whole thing made her feel weak, stupid and crazy. And now he would think she was weak, stupid and crazy.

"This happened at the same time as whatever happened that put you in protective custody?" he asked softly.

She nodded. "I've been blind for a month. The doctors say my sight could return at any time." They'd also said it was possible it might never return, but she refused to consider that possibility.

He remained silent and she continued. "I just thought you should know. I haven't had time to adjust much, so I'm not what you'd consider a high-functioning blind person." She couldn't help the bitterness, the slight ache of the unfairness of it all that colored her voice. "But we won't tell your friends that not only did you have the misfortune of falling in love with a blind woman, but a crazy one, as well.''

There was another long pause. ''Self-pity isn't very becoming.''

His words hung in the air for a long moment, and for that singular moment, she couldn't believe he'd had the audacity to accuse her of self-pity. What did he know about her life, about her?

Anger, swift and self-righteous, suddenly filled her. She stood, allowing the anger free reign. ''How dare you!'' she exclaimed. She glared in the direction she thought he stood. ''You aren't the one who has lost everything. You have no idea what I've been through...what I'm continuing to go through.''

Somewhere in the back of her mind, she knew she was overreacting, that her anger far exceeded the offense, but it was an anger that had been building inside her since the night her world had exploded apart through inexplicable violence and gut-wrenching terror.

She couldn't corral the anger now that it had been set free. It was much easier to finally give in to it, to allow it to consume her.

''You have your nice life in a nice town,'' she said, her voice strident. ''I've lost my family, my career and my sight. Excuse me if I drift momentarily into self-pity. I think I've earned the right. However, if it makes you uncomfortable, I'll take it into my room.''

She desperately wanted to make a dramatic,

graceful exit, but as she swept away from the table, she crashed into the corner with her hip, then bumped into the doorway.

Thankfully Jesse didn't reach out to help her, as if instinctively knowing she needed to leave under her own steam, even if she were black and blue by the time she reached her room.

Jesse winced as he heard her bump into the coffee table, then bang into the end table. A moment later he heard the slam of her bedroom door.

He released a sigh, and worried his hair with a sweep of his hand. He was sorry for his thoughtless words. But he had a feeling she didn't want to hear an apology at the moment.

Her family. She'd said she'd lost her family. A husband? Children? He remembered vividly his mother's grief when his father had died, a grief so debilitating, it had eventually stolen her will to live.

It was the memory of that grief that had induced Jesse to decide he'd prefer to live his life forever alone than to risk experiencing a loss so enormous. Love began with such promise, but always ended in heartache.

As he worked to clean up the dinner mess, his mind went over what little information she'd given him, provoking more questions than answers.

She was right about one thing: he didn't know what had happened to her, and he had no right to judge or censure her.

He finished cleaning the kitchen and went into the living room. His usual routine was to turn on the television and relax until bedtime. But tonight he didn't turn it on, felt as if it would be rude to do so since Cecilia couldn't watch with him.

What did Paul do in the evenings? How did he spend the dark hours of his life? These questions drifted into his head, unwelcomed and disturbing.

Jesse had made the decision years ago to walk out of his best friend Paul's life, knowing his presence would forever be a reminder of the tragedy Paul had endured.

Damn Bob Sanford for handing him this particular assignment, and damn Cecilia Webster for making him remember what he'd spent so many years trying to forget.

He paced the living room restlessly, his thoughts on Cecilia. Hysterical blindness. Jesse had never heard of such a condition, but he knew the mind was capable of many things.

He froze as he heard the guest room door open. "Jesse?"

"I'm right here," he replied as Cecilia entered the living room.

Slowly she made her way across the room to the sofa and sat. "I think I owe you an apology," she said as she folded her hands in her lap.

"No, I owe you one," he countered. He sat down opposite her. "You were right when you said I have no right to judge you or comment on where you are in your life at the moment. I don't know what's happened to you, and it's none of my business. My business is to keep you safe."

"Okay, you're right. You owe me an apology."

For the first time since she'd arrived, a small smile graced her lips. "And I accept, but only if you accept mine, as well."

"Done," he replied. She was pretty without a smile, but with her lips curved upward, she was more than pretty, and a stir of pleasure coursed through him.

"So, tell me…what do the good people of Mustang do in the evenings to pass the time?"

Jesse shrugged, then remembered she couldn't see the gesture. "We don't have a movie theater, no bowling alley or shopping mall, so entertainment is pretty limited."

Jesse realized that while he talked, he was studying her features. Society taught people that it was impolite to stare, but in this case, there was no need to look away or avert his gaze for politeness' sake.

Whatever sleep she had gotten before the interference of her disturbing nightmares had been enough to erase the circles beneath her eyes. He assumed she wore no makeup and marveled at the length of her dark lashes. She had the smoothest skin he'd ever seen, broken only by a tiny mole just above the left corner of her lips.

"Jesse?"

He realized he'd stopped talking and wondered if she'd sensed he was staring at her. "I was just gathering my thoughts," he said. Then he continued. "Most of the adults of Mustang are porch-sitters. Almost everyone has a porch swing or chairs, and on nice evenings you can hear neighbors calling back and forth to one another. Then, at about seven-thirty or so, a lot of people drift down to the diner for dessert and coffee and gossip.''

"Quite a different life-style from—'' She caught herself. "From where I come from.'' She shifted positions on the sofa and he caught a whiff of her pleasant floral perfume.

She obviously didn't trust him yet and was afraid to let him know what city held the secrets of her past and the events that had brought her to Mustang.

"Without movie theaters or shopping malls, what do the youth of Mustang do for entertainment?''

"The town holds a lot of dances and social gatherings, but most of the time the teens gather at a little stream just outside of town. There's a tree down there they call the kissing tree and legend has it if you kiss a girl beneath that tree, her heart will belong to you through eternity.''

She smiled. "Have you ever kissed a girl beneath the tree?''

"Nah. Came close a couple of times in my youth, but the idea of eternity always loomed larger than any desire to steal a kiss.'' He frowned. "At the moment, the kissing tree and the surrounding area is off-limits to everyone.''

"Why is that?''

Jesse stood, restless as he thought of the latest criminal case to strike the small town. It was the craziest crime he'd ever had to deal with. "Two weeks ago a woman was kidnapped from her bedroom in the middle of the night.'' Jesse paced from the chair to the window. "She was bound, blindfolded and gagged. Apparently she was taken to the kissing tree, kissed, then left there. She was found by a couple of teenagers.''

"How horrible. Was she hurt?'' She spoke first to the chair, then toward the window, as if unsure exactly where he stood.

"Physically, no. But she was terribly traumatized.'' He left the window and again sat in his chair, realizing it was easier for her to talk to him if he remained static. ''At first we figured it might be a bad joke, some sort of prank or bet carried out by some kid. Then last week it happened again to another single woman.''

"You still think it's kids playing jokes?''

"No.'' Jesse threaded a hand through his hair and forced himself to remain seated. ''If the females were teenagers, then I might still think another teen was responsible, but these women aren't teenagers. The first is twenty-six and the latest is twenty-eight. They aren't kids.''

"You certainly didn't need the extra responsibility of a blind woman in your care right now,'' she said, only this time he heard no tinge of self-pity in her voice. She was merely stating the obvious.

"I wouldn't have mentioned this to you at all, but if you're going to be here for any length of time, you're sure to hear about it from other sources.'' Jesse rubbed his stomach, where he thought he might be trying to develop an ulcer. ''Mustang's intrepid social reporter has decided to take it upon herself and become the reporter detailing the case of Casanova.''

His stomach burned as he thought of Millicent Creighton, who at the best of times could be an irritant, but lately had been a veritable pain in the rear. Twice in the last week, he'd caught the older woman snooping around the kissing tree, looking for clues to the "madman who held Mustang in his grip of terror." The last time he'd caught her there, he'd threatened to arrest her if he found her there again.

"Casanova...is that what you're calling him?"

"That's what our friendly reporter, Millie Creighton, has dubbed him."

She released a sigh and twisted a strand of her hair between thumb and forefinger. Jesse noticed that her hand trembled slightly. "There's really no place in this world that's truly safe, is there?"

She didn't wait for his reply, but rather continued. "You think you're safe in your own home, or in a family member's home, but there are no guarantees. You think you're safe in your own bed, but that isn't necessarily so, is it?"

Her unseeing gaze found him, her eyes luminous, yet holding the shadows of whatever nightmare she'd endured. "Tell me I'll be safe here, Jesse. I just need to know that for a little while I can let go of the fear inside me."

As Jesse saw the haunting of her eyes, felt both the tragedy and the fear that emanated from her, he wished he could reassure her, promise her sanctuary, but Jesse had never been one to make false promises.

He knew nothing about her situation, knew nothing about what danger might find her here. He wouldn't lie, couldn't give her guarantees that didn't exist.

Something—an expression of need in her eyes—touched him, and he didn't like it. He didn't like it one bit. He didn't want to get caught up in her drama, didn't want to know her life history or what had so dramatically changed her life. She was a job—nothing more, nothing less. In two weeks' time she'd be gone, back to where she belonged.

"My job is to keep you safe, and that's what I intend to do." His job wasn't to help her work through her state of blindness, nor was it to aid her in adjusting to the losses fate had thrown her way.

Still, being sure in his mind what his responsibilities were where she was concerned, didn't dispel the feeling that if he wasn't very careful, he could be in way over his head with this woman.

Chapter 3

Allison awoke to sunshine warming her face. For a moment she remained still, pretending that when she opened her eyes she'd have to squint against the brilliant morning light streaming through the window.

She'd never dreamed that one day she would miss that eye-watering, slight sting of looking directly at the sun.

She stretched languidly, realizing that despite the unfamiliarity of the bed, she'd slept well. No nightmares had come to haunt her, no dreams of any kind had disturbed her rest.

Drawing in a slow, deep breath, she thought of the conversation she'd shared with Jesse last night. She'd been seeking comfort, his absolute certainty that she would be safe while in Mustang, but he'd been unable to offer her any absolutes.

She frowned thoughtfully as she realized what she'd really wanted from Jesse was more than a mere assurance that she'd be safe in Mustang; she'd wanted him to tell her that her blindness would eventually go away, that the bad guys would be put behind bars, that she'd be able to pick up the pieces of her life and that eventually the sharp, intense heartache of losing John and Alicia would fade. She'd wanted the impossible from him.

Opening her eyes, a momentary flare of disappointment flowed through her. Darkness. Always darkness. What scared her was that with each day that passed, she expected nothing more.

She was beginning to accept her blindness, and that frightened her as much as anything.

Irritated with her thoughts, she got out of bed. Grabbing the robe that awaited her, she pulled it around her and headed for the bathroom.

She was reaching for the bathroom doorknob when the door suddenly flew open, throwing her off balance. She stumbled forward.

"Whoa," Jesse exclaimed. He grabbed her by the shoulders and her hands found the broad expanse of his chest.

Her senses filled with the scent of him, the utterly male, overwhelmingly enticing fragrance of spicy soap and shaving cream. At the same time, her fingertips registered the fevered warmth of his skin and the strength of the smooth muscles beneath.

For one crazy moment she wanted to lay her head against his chest, feel those strong muscles beneath her cheek, listen to the rhythm of his heart beating as his arms enfolded her tightly.

She stepped back, still slightly off balance as she quickly pulled her hands from his chest, as if flames of fire danced just beneath the surface of his skin.

His hands remained on her shoulders and she could feel their warmth penetrating the thin material of her robe. "You okay?" he asked, his voice huskier than usual as he finally dropped his hands.

"Fine. I just got off balance for a moment." She felt the blush of her cheeks. She pulled her robe more tightly around her, hoping desperately that she was sufficiently covered. "I'll go back to my room...."

"No, I'm finished in here. I'll just get out of your way," he said, and brushed past her into the hallway. "What would you like for breakfast?"

"Just coffee is fine. I'm not much of a morning eater."

"Ah, your loss. I make a mean omelet."

"Okay, maybe just a small one." She smiled. "A woman has a right to change her mind, right?"

He laughed, the deep sound permeating through her. "From what I understand about women, it's the one thing you can count on." He hesitated a moment. "You need help getting to the kitchen?"

She shook her head. "I'll manage."

A few moments later, standing beneath the warm spray of the shower, she thought of her words. She'd manage. Perhaps it was time to stop wishing her blindness away and learn to manage what fate had handed her.

She could learn Braille, buy a computer program that would talk so she could write letters and such. There were all kinds of products available to help the visually impaired.

No! Her mind rejected the thought. Some place deep inside her was the superstitious fear that if she learned to cope with her blindness, then fate would keep her forever blind. She didn't want to cope. She didn't want to manage. She wanted to see. She wanted her life back.

Leaning her head beneath the brunt of the spray, she allowed shampoo and thoughts of blindness to drain away. Instead, her mind replayed that moment when her hands had touched Jesse's chest.

Heat rushed through her at the memory.

She wished she'd had an hour to explore the muscled contours and smooth skin, wished her fingers could have taken the time to give her the mental picture that her eyes couldn't provide.

Shutting off the water, she pulled the shower curtain open and reached for the towel near the sink, her mind still filled with thoughts of Jesse.

She pulled her robe back on and left the bathroom. In her room, she quickly dressed in a pair of jeans and a T-shirt.

As she brushed her hair, she recognized her vulnerability with Jesse. It would be easy to fall into some sort of demented romantic fantasy where he was concerned. He was her protector, her single contact with the world at large. Where Keller had been cold and impersonal, Jesse exuded a warmth that was appealing.

However, she couldn't forget that, to him, she was an assignment. Nothing more. Nothing less. Besides, she thought with a touch of bitterness, what man in his right mind would want to saddle himself with a helpless blind woman? A blind woman who several Templeton cops would love to see dead.

All the lessons her mother had taught her about independence and self-reliance replayed in her mind—needing a man was a weakness not to be tolerated. She'd lectured over and over again that ultimately a woman could only depend on herself for survival, and depending on a man for anything was the work of a fool.

Allison ran a hand over her hair, feeling for errant strands. Satisfied that she looked presentable, she left the bedroom, deciding that she'd indulged herself in deep thought for entirely too long, especially considering the fact that she had yet to have a cup of coffee.

As she entered the kitchen, she drew in a deep breath of the luscious scents that permeated the room. The fragrance of fresh brewed coffee battled with browning sausage and onion. "Something smells wonderful," she said as she eased into the same chair she'd sat in the night before.

"I love breakfast. Coffee?" Jesse's voice came from someplace to the right of her.

"Please."

"Cream or sugar?"

"No, just black." She heard the sound of a cup being set in front of her. "Thanks." She reached out with both hands and wrapped her fingers around a sturdy ceramic mug.

"The omelets will be ready in just a few minutes," he said. "Did you sleep well?"

"Like a baby." She took a sip of her coffee. "How about you?"

"I almost always sleep like a baby."

She took another drink of her coffee, enjoying the warmth of the sun at her back. "It's a beautiful morning, isn't it?"

"Yeah, it is. How—how did you know?"

She smiled as she heard the surprise in his voice. "Don't worry, I'm not a psychic. There must be a large window near my bed. I could feel the sun shining on me this morning."

"It's a typical gorgeous Mustang day," he said, and set a plate in front of her.

She waited until she heard his chair scoot across the tile and knew he was seated across from her at the table. "A typical gorgeous Mustang day," she repeated with amusement. "You make Mustang sound like Camelot." She picked up her fork and attempted to cut off a mouthful of the omelet.

"It's as close to Camelot as you can get," he replied. Again an easy amusement lightened his voice, an amusement that was wonderfully attractive. "It only rains after sundown and July and August may not get too hot."

Allison laughed in delight. "You know the song," she said. Who would have thought a sheriff from Montana would know the title song of a Broadway show?

"My senior year in high school, the drama department put on *Camelot*. In order to graduate, all seniors had to work on the production in some capacity or another." He paused a moment, then continued. "I made my debut as a thespian in *Camelot*."

"Really? What role did you play? King Arthur? Lancelot?"

He laughed. "Nothing quite so illustrious. I was one of the knights of the Round Table who didn't have a single line of dialogue. I just wore cardboard armor and looked pure and knightly."

"It must have been fun," she said, wistful at the thought of all the high school experiences she'd missed out on. "Our school did plays, but I never got to participate."

"Why?"

She paused a moment to take another bite of the omelet, her thoughts winging backward to her adolescence and teen years. "My sister and I were raised to believe that extracurricular activities were a waste of time. School was for an education to pursue whatever career would be our livelihood. Spare time was used for jobs to save money for college. There was no time for glee club, or football games, or dating or plays."

"Sounds pretty dismal," he said, no censure or judgment in his voice.

"It was," she admitted. "Although I understand now what motivated my mother. She was twenty when my father walked out on her—on us. She had two babies less than a year apart in age and no education or job."

"Did you ever hear from your father again?" he asked.

"No. I don't even remember him. I was only a year old when he left." She paused a moment to sip her coffee. "Anyway, Mother worked like a demon to support us. At the same time she went to college and got a degree in accounting. By the time Alicia and I were in high school, my mother had a very successful accounting business with four people working for her. But she never forgot those years of struggle, and she was determined we'd never have to go through similar experiences, that both of us would be able to survive without a man."

Allison released a slightly bitter laugh. "Thank goodness my mother isn't alive to see me now. I'm not exactly excelling in the self-sufficiency department."

"Don't be so hard on yourself," he said, his voice gentle.

She forced a smile. "You just don't want to send me to my room for indulging in self-pity."

His hand touched hers. It was a light touch, yet held warmth and comfort. There had been little solace in her life for the past month. The hospital staff she'd come in contact with had been efficient, the few law-enforcement officers she'd spoken with had been impersonal and demanding.

The comfort in Jesse's touch broke through the self-control she'd fought so hard to maintain and tapped into the grief that had yet to be fully expressed. She grabbed his hand and squeezed tightly.

"They killed her," she whispered, her voice hoarse with emotion that ripped at her heart. "They killed my sister and my brother-in-law. They shot them while I was hidden in the closet."

Tears burned at her eyes, choked in the back of her throat, but she swallowed against them as the horror of the trauma replayed itself in her mind. "I did nothing to help them. I stayed in the closet and watched John and Alicia die."

As she remembered the final gasp of Alicia's life, recalled her sister's blood on her face and her chest, she felt Jesse squeeze her hand more tightly.

The warmth of his touch met up with the coldness of her grief, creating a tumultuous tornado of emotions she could no longer contain.

Deep sobs tore through her as her heart constricted with a pain so great, she thought she might die from it. It was the grief of loss...and the guilt of survival.

She had pushed her emotions aside for weeks, focusing on the loss of her sight rather than confront the overwhelming pain of the loss of her family. Now that pain riveted through her like a hot poker stabbing her heart, searing her soul.

She was vaguely aware of Jesse removing his hand from hers. Somewhere in the back of her mind she knew she was making a spectacle of herself and probably alienating Jesse, but she could no more stop the grief than she could go back and stop the bullets that had ripped her life apart.

* * *

In his years as sheriff, Jesse had faced many things, including drunk men with guns, a scared teenage bank robber and a vicious rabid dog, but nothing in his years of experience prepared him for dealing with her tears.

Helplessly he watched her fall apart, aware that nothing he could say would possibly comfort or touch the deep anguish that obviously pummeled her. His heart ached for her.

As Cecilia's sobs grew deeper, more harsh, he stood. Not knowing if he was right or wrong, he touched her shoulder then pulled her out of her chair and into his arms.

She came to him willingly, as if needing to be held. She wrapped her arms around his neck and hid her face in the center of his chest as she wept uncontrollably.

Jesse rubbed a hand down her back and tried to ignore how sweet she smelled, the intimacy of her body pressed so tightly against his. "It's all right. You're safe now," he whispered as he patted her back.

Beneath the comforting press of her breasts against his chest, he could feel the beating of her heart. He continued to soothe her with soft words, at the same time patting her back in a rhythmic cadence that mirrored the pace of her heartbeats.

Finally her sobs began to ease, but still she clung to him as if he were a lifeline in a sea of tears. Jesse felt her heartbeat slow, returning to a more normal pace. Her weeping halted altogether, but still she remained in the circle of his arms.

She raised her head, as if to look at him. Her lashes were still damp, long dark spikes that emphasized the beauty of her eyes despite their slight redness. "Thank you," she whispered with a tremulous smile. "That had been building for a while."

"Tears are supposed to be cathartic," he replied. "You want to talk about it some more?" he asked. He wished she'd move away as he felt himself responding in a decidedly unwanted way. But she remained unmoving, her lower body still pressed against his.

"In a minute. What I'd like to do right now... I'd like to know what you look like." She removed her arms from around his neck and instead placed a hand on either side of his face. "I can only see you through touch. Do you mind?"

Before he could reply, her fingertips moved across his forehead, down the bridge of his nose, then across his eyes. Slowly, deliberately, her cool fingers explored the contours of his face, each touch evoking heat inside him.

"What color are your eyes?" she asked, her breath warm on his face. He realized his heart was now beating a rhythm faster than normal.

"Blue."

She nodded, and continued her exploration of his facial features. Slowly, methodically, her hands continued to work.

When her fingers danced across his lips, he fought an impulse to open his mouth and kiss her fingertips. He breathed in relief when she moved to his hair.

"Black," he said, answering the question before she could verbalize it.

"Thank you," she said, and finally stepped back from him. "I'm sorry about ruining your breakfast."

"You didn't ruin anything," he replied. "I'd already finished my omelet when you got upset. So, you want to talk? You don't have to," he added hurriedly. "It's not imperative that you tell me anything. I understand if you don't trust me."

"Trust you?" She smiled ruefully. "If I can't trust you, then I'm utterly lost. I'd like you to know what happened. I think maybe I need to talk about it."

"Why don't we go into the living room?" he suggested. In there he could gain enough distance from her that he wouldn't be able to smell her sweet fragrance. Physical distance would provide emotional distance, and at the moment that's exactly what he needed.

In the living room, she sat on the sofa and Jesse sank into the chair facing her. He watched the emotions that played across her face as she rubbed her forehead and prepared to share with him the events that had destroyed life as she knew it.

"It wasn't unusual for me to spend the evening with my sister, Alicia, and her husband, John." She placed her hands in her lap, her fingers laced together. Her knuckles were slightly whitened by the tension that held her unnaturally stiff. "This particular night was like a hundred others, except that instead of driving my car to their place, I took a cab.''

''Why?'' he asked with a cop's curiosity.

''I was tired and Alicia had told me earlier in the day that she'd bought the makings of strawberry daiquiris and I didn't want to have to worry about driving home after having a couple of drinks.''

She frowned and her knuckles appeared to whiten even more as she continued. ''If only I'd driven my car. If only my car had been parked out front....'' Her voice trailed off.

''Don't go there,'' Jesse said softly, knowing well how easily self-recriminations could destroy a person.

She nodded, then continued. ''I had been in the house just a few minutes when we heard a car pull up out front. John looked out the window and told me to get in the closet.'' Her frown deepened. ''Any other time I would have balked at the suggestion, but something in his tone of voice made me obey without question. John and Alicia were police officers, and John often worked undercover, so I thought perhaps he was worried about whoever was there seeing me.''

She pulled her hands apart and stood, as if finding it impossible to sit still while she told the full story. Jesse leaned forward and pulled the coffee table away from the sofa, giving her room to pace without danger of bumping her knees.

''Two men came in the front door, and the minute I saw them, I almost stepped out of the closet.

The two men were police officers.'' She raised a hand to push a strand of hair off her face, and Jesse noticed her hand trembled.

She paced the space in front of the sofa, the tight jeans displaying her slender legs. "But before I could open the closet door and step out, the two men shot John and Alicia.'' Her voice rose slightly and she stopped walking and drew a deep breath, as if to marshal her emotions.

Jesse realized he was holding his breath. Two cops, murdered by two other cops. No wonder Bob Sanford and Kent Keller had immediately whisked her away. It was an ugly scenario.

"Apparently I passed out in the closet. When I came to, I was blind and in a hospital room. That's when I met Bob Sanford, who explained to me that John and Alicia had been working for Internal Affairs and investigating a group of dirty cops.''

"And apparently the dirty cops learned of IA's investigation and John and Alicia's part in it,'' Jesse said.

She nodded. "And now John and Alicia are dead, and the good guys are hoping my sight will return so I can identify the two men who killed them.''

"Can you identify them?''

She sank down to the sofa once again. "Oh, yes. Their faces are burned into my mind. Unfortunately, at the moment I'm a blind witness.''

"And what happens if you never regain your sight?'' He could tell the question pained her as she winced.

She straightened her back. "I refuse to consider that possibility."

He heard the strength of conviction in her voice, but he also heard an underlying fear.

He decided to leave that particular topic alone. "You mentioned a *group* of dirty cops... Did anyone tell you how many were in the group?"

"Bob Sanford told me there are eight. The Renegade Eight is what they call themselves. Unfortunately, nobody seems to know exactly who the eight are." She forced a smile in his direction. "It seems I have a small posse probably seeking my whereabouts and praying for my death."

"Don't worry, little lady, the sheriff of Mustang knows how to handle a posse of desperadoes." Jesse did his best John Wayne imitation, and was rewarded by her laughter.

"Performing that kind of a bad imitation would definitely make desperadoes run for the hills," she said. "We're a long way from Chicago—that's where I'm from. Surely nobody could track me all the way here."

Jesse frowned. He wasn't so sure. He knew as well as anyone that cops could be quite resourceful when it came to seeking out information they wanted. Knowing there may be as many as eight dirty cops seeking her, definitely was a sobering thought.

If three people knew where she was, that was two too many. He wouldn't feel comfortable until he got word that the eight cops had been arrested and put behind bars.

"Do you want to know my real name?" she asked.

"No," Jesse hurriedly replied. "I don't think it's a good idea for you to tell me. I might accidentally call you by that name in front of other people. It's best that you remain Cecilia Webster to me."

"Okay," she agreed, although he thought he detected disappointment in the single word.

"What did you do before all this?" he asked, attempting to get her mind off bad guys, killer cops and false identities.

She smiled, and he saw the tension slowly leaving her. "I'm an interior decorator."

He groaned. "I think I'm glad you can't see this place. It would probably give you nightmares."

"It can't be that bad," she protested. "What's your color scheme?"

"Color scheme?"

She leaned forward, her features lit with an animation he hadn't seen before, an animation that transformed her from pretty to something far more powerful. "You know, what's the dominant color of the room?"

Jesse shrugged and looked around. "I've got a brown-and-orange sofa, beige carpeting, a rose-colored chair. I'm not sure there is a dominant color."

"Orange sofa and rose-colored chair?" She looked slightly ill. "You've just managed to do what nothing and nobody has done in the past month."

"What's that?" he asked.

"You almost made me grateful I'm blind." The animation still shone on her features, and a stir of desire winged through Jesse, both appalling and irritating him. "I'll tell you what I'll do," she continued. "As soon as I get my sight back and everything is settled, I'll come back here to Mustang and redecorate your house."

"It's a deal," Jesse agreed easily, although he knew it was a false promise on her part. This was a place to hide, a state of limbo for her.

When her sight returned and her life was no longer threatened, she would go back to Chicago and never look back. He knew that he and Mustang, Montana, would simply represent part of a very bad dream she would never again want to revisit.

Chapter 4

Sheriff Jesse Wilder had lied to her, Allison thought as she sat on the sofa and listened to the sounds of him clearing the table and cleaning up the breakfast dishes.

He'd told her he wasn't particularly good-looking, but her fingertips had told her something altogether different.

Even now, her fingers still held the memory of his skin and features. His face was slender, with high cheekbones and a straight nose. He had long lashes and she could easily see in her mind his blue eyes framed by the dark fringes.

His mouth was soft, achingly soft, and if she dwelled on it, it would be far too easy to imagine those lips pressed against hers.

She stirred restlessly and smiled as she heard him

whistling "Camelot" as he worked. She could imagine his dark hair falling carelessly over his forehead as he rinsed the dishes. She knew from touching that his hair was thick and silky and she had a feeling he needed a haircut.

When she put all the single images together, what she got was a mental image of a handsome man.

A confirmed bachelor, she reminded herself. Not that she was interested. She had a life, a full life waiting for her return to Chicago. That was her Camelot.

"Want another cup of coffee?" Jesse called from the kitchen.

"No, thanks. I'm fine," she replied. She heard him enter the room and smiled in his general direction.

"I thought maybe we'd eat lunch down at the café this afternoon," he said. She heard the squeak of a cushion and knew he'd sat in the chair opposite the sofa.

"Are you sure that's a good idea?" The thought of going out, of being vulnerable, sent a flutter of anxiety to the pit of her stomach.

"Keller told me to keep my routine as normal as possible and to tell everyone you're my girlfriend. Every person in town will begin to wonder about you if I keep you isolated here. That wouldn't be normal." He sighed audibly. "Besides, trust me that we'll know if a stranger shows up anywhere in the vicinity. A fly doesn't land on the back of a dog, that somebody in this town doesn't comment about it five minutes later."

She laughed, her anxiety ebbing somewhat. She had to trust his judgment, had to believe that he not only knew his hometown and the people in it, but also knew the business of protection. "Okay, lunch out sounds good." She jumped as a heavy knock fell on the front door.

Jesse got up and walked to the window. "Relax, it's my deputy," he said to her, then opened the door. "Hi, Vic, what's up?"

"Jesse, I think we've got another one." The deputy's voice boomed loud and deep.

"Dammit!" Jesse exclaimed. "Who?"

"Maggie Watson. I don't know, Jesse. She's in bad shape. She's locked herself in her house and won't let anyone in."

"Has she been hurt physically?" Allison heard the concern in Jesse's voice.

"Nobody knows. Amanda Creighton came down to the office and said something was wrong with Maggie, that she and Maggie were supposed to meet this morning at the café for coffee. When Maggie didn't show up, Amanda went to her house." The deputy paused, apparently to draw breath. "Maggie wouldn't let her in the house, but she says she is a victim of Casanova. I don't know what's going on, but it sounds like she's freaked out totally."

"Okay, you go on back to the office and I'll check things out at Maggie's place," Jesse said briskly. "You might try to find Shelly. Maybe Maggie will feel more comfortable talking to a woman deputy."

"Shelly left early this morning to visit her parents. By this time she's miles and miles away from here."

Allison listened with interest as the two men finished their discussion and Vic left the house. She tilted her head questioningly, aware that Jesse hadn't moved from the door. "I'll be fine, Jesse. Go where you're needed."

"I'm not comfortable leaving you here alone." He hesitatcd a moment, then continued. "Why don't you ride along with me? I can't promise you how long we'll be gone and I'll ask that you remain in the car, but I'd feel more comfortable if you don't stay here alone."

"Okay," she agreed, and stood. It didn't much matter to her whether she sat in his car or sat on his sofa.

Moments later she was safely ensconced in the passenger seat of Jesse's car. "Who's Maggie?" she asked.

"Maggie is a twenty-eight-year-old who works the evening shift as a waitress at the Round-Up."

"And the Round-Up is?"

"A bar at the outskirts of town, decorated like an old-fashioned saloon."

Allison nodded and sank deeper into the plush leather seat. "Your car is new."

"How did you know that?" he asked with a note of incredulity. "It's less than a month old."

She smiled. "It still has that new smell."

He sniffed. "I can't smell it anymore."

"I guess it's true that senses compensate for each

other when one no longer works. I've noticed in the last month both my hearing and my sense of smell seem to be more acute.''

"Let's hope Maggie's sense of smell and hearing were working overtime while she was with Casanova." He pulled to a stop. "We're in front of Maggie's house now. I'm going to see if I can get her to come out. You just sit tight." His car door opened then closed, and Allison knew she was alone in the car.

She rolled down her window, letting in not only the sweet scent of summer, but Jesse's voice, as well.

"Maggie, come on. Open the door and talk to me," Jesse said, his tone soft and pleading.

"No." The female voice was muffled, but audible to Allison. "I don't want to talk to anyone. Just leave me alone." Apparently Maggie was talking through an open window.

"I can't do that," Jesse replied. "We need to talk. I need to file a report."

"I don't want to talk to you. I just want to be left alone." Maggie's voice rose both in volume and in tone. "I don't want anyone to see me. I feel ugly and dirty. Go away!"

She didn't want anyone to see her. Allison frowned thoughtfully, then before the impulse could pass, she opened her car door and stepped out. "Jesse?" she called hesitantly.

He walked toward her, his footsteps brisk on the surface of the sidewalk. "She won't let me in," he said when he stood close enough to Allison that she could feel his presence. "Something is wrong. This doesn't feel like the other two."

"What do you mean?"

"The other women were upset, scared and traumatized, but not to this level. I've got a bad feeling."

"Why don't you let me try? Maybe she'll let me in."

"Why would she? She doesn't even know you," he said.

"And that's exactly why she might talk to me," Allison countered. "It's worth a try, isn't it?"

Jesse sighed, then took Allison by the hand. "Okay, we'll give it a try."

He guided her down the sidewalk toward the house. "There are three steps up to the porch," he instructed. She nodded and took the steps carefully, intensely aware of the heat of his hand on her elbow, the evocative scent of his cologne. "Okay, the front door is about three steps straight ahead." He released his hold on her.

Allison drew a deep breath and walked the three paces to the door. She knocked softly. "Maggie? My name is Cecilia Webster. I'm a friend of Jesse's. Could I come in? Would you talk to me?"

"Please, just go away and leave me alone." Maggie's voice was filled with anguish and her deep suffering touched Allison's heart.

She knew what it was like to be tormented, to feel dirty and ugly. It was exactly how she felt each time she thought of the night of John's and Alicia's deaths. It was the same way she felt when she awakened each day to her blindness, a blindness induced by her inability to cope, by the weakness of her character.

"Maggie, if you let me in to talk to you, I won't be able to look at you. I'm blind." Allison held her breath as silence greeted her words.

The silence stretched immeasurably long, and defeat weighed heavy on Allison's shoulders. Jesse stepped beside Allison and touched her arm, as if to tell her to forget it.

"Is this some kind of a trick?" Maggie's voice broke the stifling silence.

"No trick," Jesse replied. "Cecilia is blind."

Again silence.

Allison held her breath, her heart pounding anxiously. The breeze that had been softly blowing stopped, as if all of nature held its breath, as well.

Allison could feel the other woman's hurt, her fear and her irrational shame wafting through the door. An audible click cut through the stillness, the click of the door being unlocked.

"Cecilia can come in...but only her," Maggie said.

Jesse's fingers tightened on Allison's arm. "I have to talk to her. You have to get her to agree to let me in."

Allison nodded, then reached for the doorknob. She opened the door, but remained standing on the threshold. "Maggie?" She held out a hand. "You'll have to help me."

It felt as if she waited for an eternity. Finally a

cold, trembling hand grasped hers. "Maybe we could sit on the sofa," Maggie said.

"That would be fine," Allison replied and allowed herself to be led across the room. Five steps to the sofa, Allison calculated. When the two women were seated, Maggie drew her hand away and again silence reigned.

"You want to tell me what happened?" Allison asked gently.

A deep wrenching sob was the woman's reply. Allison felt the sob clear down in her toes, and with the compassion of a fellow victim, she reached out and embraced Maggie.

Initially Maggie stiffened and held herself erect. But as another sob choked in her throat, she melted against Allison and cried.

For several minutes, Allison held her and soothed her, allowing her to vent the emotions that ripped through her. "Maggie, you have to tell me what happened," she said when Maggie's sobs had eased somewhat.

Maggie released one final, shuddering gasp, then straightened and pulled away from Allison's embrace. "In the middle of the night, somebody came into my room. He blindfolded me and gagged me, then tied me up and threw me over his shoulder."

Her voice was soft, nearly inaudible and Allison sensed the tenuous grasp she had on her control. "Maggie, before you tell me anything more, couldn't you let Jesse come in? He needs to hear this so he can catch whoever did this to you."

"Okay," she conceded, although another sob caught in her throat. "But just Jesse. Nobody else."

Allison stood and slowly walked the five paces back to the front door. She opened it and Jesse stumbled into her.

"She says you can come in," Allison told him as he grabbed her hand. She lowered her voice to a whisper. "Be gentle, Jesse. She's very fragile."

He squeezed her hand. "Thanks." With him still holding her hand, they moved back into the mainroom. Maggie was once again softly weeping.

Allison rejoined her on the sofa while Jesse remained standing. Allison reached for Maggie's hand as Jesse began to question her.

As she listened to Jesse inquire about the previous night's events, she marveled at his smooth, calming tone, the compassion and support he offered Maggie.

Allison was drawn to him like she'd been drawn to no other man. Was it because he was not only attractive with a broad, hard chest, but also seemed to be a genuinely nice guy? Or, was her attraction based solely on the fact that she was blind and vulnerable, and he was her sole security in an alien world?

Was it a mysterious chemical reaction at work within her, attracting her to Jesse like an ocean seeks the shore, or would she have been attracted to anyone who was kind to her in these hours of need?

For all she knew, had she remained in Keller's care for a few more days, she might have entertained fantasies about him. She frowned as she thought of the cold, distant man. No way, she scoffed.

Still, she knew better than to trust anything she might feel toward Jesse. Nothing was real in her life at the moment, not even the name she was known by.

She had to remember that she was living a fantasy existence provided to ensure her safety. Nothing she experienced here in Mustang had anything at all to do with her real life back in Chicago.

She focused again on the conversation between Maggie and Jesse.

"When he got you to the kissing tree, what happened?" Jesse asked.

"He put me on the ground…and kissed my cheek…then he…he—" She broke off, sobbing once again.

Allison squeezed her hand, willing her the strength to get through the trauma of telling aloud what had happened to her. Maggie's hand gripped Allison's so tightly, pain radiated up her arm.

"He…he ripped the tape from my ankles….and then he…he raped me."

Allison heard Jesse's swift intake of breath at the same time shock riveted through her. It would seem that Casanova had degenerated from a female-kissing crazy to a rapist.

It was nearly seven when Jesse led Cecilia into the café for a bite to eat. Weariness weighed heavily on his shoulders as he guided Cecilia to a booth in the back of the room.

It had been a long, disturbing day. After taking a statement from Maggie, Jesse and Cecilia had taken her to the hospital where she'd undergone a physical examination and some crisis counseling.

Jesse had contacted Amanda Creighton, Maggie's best friend, to come and stay with her, then he and Cecilia had driven out to the scene of the crime.

While Cecilia sat patiently in the car, Jesse looked for physical evidence that might point him to the perpetrator. Casanova, whoever he was, was smart. He was smart enough to leave nothing behind—no footprints, no cloth snagged on branches or brush, no cigarette butts or gum wrappers. Nothing to give a single clue to his identity.

The only thing Jesse had as evidence was the duct tape Casanova used to bind his victims. Ordinary duct tape was sold in a half-dozen stores in Mustang, and hundreds of thousands of stores around the country. He'd packaged the tape in evidence bags and sent it to the crime lab in Butte, hoping for fingerprints, but certain there would be none. Maggie, as well as the other two victims of Casanova, had been certain he'd worn gloves.

Jesse opened the menu, then looked at Cecilia. "The special tonight is meat loaf and mashed potatoes, with a choice of two vegetables."

"Sounds fine," she said without enthusiasm, as if she didn't much care what she ate, but knew she needed to refuel.

He felt the same way. He had no appetite, but knew he had to eat something. Breakfast that morning seemed a lifetime ago.

When the waitress—a giggling high school student working part-time—arrived, he ordered their meals, then leaned back in the cracked leather booth and released a sigh of exhaustion.

"Long day," Cecilia said, as if his sigh had come from her.

"Yeah. Long and frustrating." He leaned forward and stared at Cecilia for a long moment. She looked as tired as he felt. Her face was pale and a faint wrinkle creased her forehead.

His mind flashed with a picture of how she'd looked when he'd met her at the bathroom door that morning. For just a moment, he'd been mortified, aware that he was clad only in a pair of boxers. Then he'd remembered that she couldn't see him and he'd relaxed somewhat.

Still, he'd been able to see her. He'd noticed her sleep-tousled hair, the drowsiness that darkened her eyes. She'd been wearing a pale blue nightgown and a matching robe. The silky material had been cool to his touch as he'd grabbed her shoulders, but had quickly warmed beneath his fingers. She'd looked tender, inviting and sexy as hell.

In a single instant, he'd wondered what it would be like to awaken each morning with her next to him in his bed. The thought had been fleeting and instantly dismissed. He didn't want a woman—he didn't want anyone in his life.

"Jesse?"

"Yeah, I'm here. Just thinking." He had a feeling she sensed him staring at her. He looked down at the top of the table and thought back over the events of the afternoon. "I don't know what I would have done without you today. I don't think Maggie would have ever talked to me without your help."

She picked up her napkin and unfolded it in her lap. "I'm glad I could be some help."

"You were more than help. You were Maggie's lifeline." He thought of how Maggie had clung to Cecilia not only through the initial interview phase, but Maggie had also insisted Cecilia be with her during the physical exam.

"Maybe victims somehow recognize each other and Maggie knew instinctively that I'm a soul mate when it comes to suffering senseless violence."

"Maybe," he agreed. "But I think it has to do with the fact that you were really good with her. She trusted you. If your sight never returns, you could always get a job working with people."

The frown on her forehead deepened. "My sight *will* return and I'll go back to running my shop and decorating homes." Her voice trembled slightly, as if she were afraid to consider that her sight might not return.

Had Paul fought against his blindness? Had he refused to accept what fate—what Jesse had handed him? Jesse pushed away thoughts of Paul. He had enough on his mind without adding in ancient history.

"Here we are," Trish, the youthful waitress,

said, arriving at their table with their drinks. "Coffee for Sheriff Wilder, and iced tea for his lady friend."

"Thanks, Trish." Jesse wrapped his hands around the coffee mug, hoping some of the heat would seep into his bones, bones weary and cold with thoughts of a rapist terrorizing the town he loved.

"Amanda Creighton seemed like a nice woman," Cecilia said.

"Yeah, Amanda's great. She'll stay with Maggie as long as Maggie needs her there. We've got a town full of great people, people who rally around one another when there's trouble." Again frustration swept through him as he thought of the young women of Mustang, women he apparently couldn't protect.

She reached across the table, nearly upending his coffee. "Oops, sorry," she said, a blush coloring her cheeks. "I was looking for your hand."

"It's right here." He touched her hand and she wrapped her fingers around his.

"This isn't your fault, Jesse. You can't blame yourself for the actions of an obviously sick person."

"True, but I can blame myself for not taking the first two incidents seriously enough."

"There's a big difference between a kiss beneath the kissing tree and rape," she said, her fingers sending rivulets of warmth through him. "You couldn't know that Casanova would move from kissing to this."

He broke the contact. "That's what bothers me. The way I see it, there are two possible scenarios. Either Casanova has made the stakes higher, or there's a copycat at work."

"A copycat?"

"It's possible." A sick feeling roiled through Jesse as he thought of not one, but two nuts preying on the women of Mustang. "Thanks to Amanda's mother, Millicent Creighton, our intrepid reporter, most of the details of the first two crimes were in the paper. It would have been relatively easy for somebody to duplicate those incidences and take them one step further." His stomach burned as his mind worked to assess how to catch the culprit before another woman got hurt.

He stopped talking as Trish appeared with their meals. As Trish once again departed, Jesse sighed in frustration. "Let's drop the subject and eat," he said.

She nodded and for a few minutes they ate in silence. He watched her acquaint herself with her food, sticking a fork first in the meat loaf, then in the mashed potatoes, as if to orient herself as to where exactly each item was on her plate.

It had been easy throughout the day to temporarily forget her blindness. During the day he'd watched her offer Maggie emotional support, evoking in her the courage to get through the process each victim of a violent crime was required to go through. Cecilia had functioned with confidence and poise during the long hours of the day.

But now, watching her carefully maneuvering her

food on her fork, he was once again struck by her utter vulnerability, her total dependence upon him.

The rest of their meal was accompanied by small talk.

They spoke of the weather, and favorite baseball teams. They talked about the trials and tribulations of high school, but no matter what the topic, Jesse couldn't get his mind off Casanova and the new threat he posed to the women of Mustang.

"Maybe I should try to get in touch with Keller," he said after they'd eaten and they were lingering over coffee.

"See if he can put you someplace else." He raked a hand through his hair and his frustration flew free. "How in the hell am I supposed to keep you safe when I can't even keep the women of Mustang safe?"

"Jesse." Again her hand sought and found his on the tabletop. "Even if you do call Keller, I won't leave with him." Again Jesse felt evocative heat filling him as she tightened her grip on his hand.

"Jesse," she repeated. She leaned forward, and he felt himself doing the same, as if drawn by a dynamic force too powerful to ignore. "I trust you, Jesse. I trust you with my life. You'll find and arrest Casanova, and you'll keep me safe."

"Sheriff Wilder…just the man I'm looking for." The strident female voice caused Jesse to snap back in his seat, release Cecilia's hand and stifle a groan beneath his breath.

"Evening, Millicent," he replied.

As always, Millicent had on one of her infamous

hats. The hats were her trademark, crazy homemade concoctions that were surprisingly fanciful. Jesse tried to focus on her plump face and not on the headpiece adorned with what appeared to be real, growing petunias.

"I just came from Maggie Watson's house," Millicent said, her cheeks flushed with color. "We have a madman loose in Mustang and I want to know what I should tell my readers you're doing about it."

"Tell your readers that we're doing everything we can to assure their safety, but they should take some precautions for themselves." He paused as Millicent scrambled in her purse for a pen and the yellow pad she always carried.

"Shoot," she said with a curt nod.

Jesse grimaced. The woman had obviously seen too many movies. "Doors and windows should be locked at all times. Unmarried women should arrange to have friends sleep over, or go to somebody else's house until we resolve this."

"Thank you." Millicent placed her pad and pen back in her purse and smiled. "And now that's out of the way, I want to meet your fiancée."

"My—"

Before Jesse could protest, Millicent grabbed Cecilia's hand. "Millicent Creighton, and you're Cecilia Webster. The whole town has been buzzing all afternoon about you and Jesse. Everyone is so excited that finally somebody managed to snag this wily man's heart." She turned and looked at Jesse.

"And it's good to see the light of love softening your ugly mug."

"Ugly mug? I guess what they say about love being blind is true," Cecilia said.

A burst of laughter exploded from Millicent. "Oh, my... He didn't have a chance, did he?" she said merrily. "Not only beautiful, but a sense of humor to boot." She rocked back on her heels and looked first at Cecilia, then at Jesse. "So when's the date?"

Jesse felt a sinking sensation in the pit of his stomach. Things were spinning out of control. "The date?" he echoed.

"Everyone wants to know," Millicent exclaimed. "It's just what this town needs to take everyone's minds off the horrible Casanova business. So, tell me, when is the wedding date?"

Chapter 5

"But we aren't—"

"We haven't—"

Allison and Jesse sputtered at the same time, but their protests were as effectual as spit on the arid desert against Millicent's overwhelming enthusiasm.

"Dear girl, you must get Marissa Crockett to do your flowers. She's our florist and she does absolutely gorgeous work. And Virginia Washington does catering. She's old and doesn't do anything fancy, mind you, but her prices are fair and the food is good and hearty. A September wedding would be lovely and would give us just enough time to really do it right."

"Slow down," Jesse exclaimed the moment Millicent paused to take an audible breath. "We, uh, we haven't set a date yet."

Allison knew things were getting out of hand. In the space of an afternoon she'd transformed from a girlfriend to a fiancée. But she kept her mouth shut, allowing Jesse to handle the crazy situation and the overeager reporter who smelled of lavender and, strangely enough, potting soil.

"Now is a perfect time to set the date. I can put a notice in the social pages." Millicent once again gripped Allison's hand. "Honey, you'll make a lovely September bride. I can just see you with the flush of fall in the air."

"Okay, how about September 25? Is that all right with you, honey?" Jesse asked, his voice tight with irritation.

Allison sat up straighter in the booth, surprised by Jesse's question. "Sure," she agreed.

"Wonderful!" Millicent squeezed Allison's hand. "You'll be a lovely addition to our little town." She dropped Allison's hand. "And now I'd better get over to the newspaper office and turn in my columns for tomorrow's edition. Sheriff, I'll be in touch about these horrid crimes."

"She's gone," Jesse said after a moment of silence.

"Is she always so...so..." Allison fumbled for an adjective.

"Pushy? Maddening? Irritating? Yes. I can't believe that woman had a petunia on her head."

"Excuse me?" Allison frowned in confusion.

Jesse chuckled. "Millicent wears hats," he explained. "Hats she makes herself. They're sort of her trademark and they're always a little weird and outrageous. Today she had on a hat with a real petunia growing out of it.''

"That explains why she smelled like potting soil,'' Allison exclaimed with a laugh, then sobered as she realized how complicated their cover story had suddenly grown. "You didn't have enough on your mind—you needed to add in a pending wedding, as well?''

"I figured if I didn't give Millicent a date, she'd never leave us alone. It was easier to just give her what she wanted.''

"So, when it comes time for me to leave, will it be because you sent me away, or because I called off the wedding? In other words, will I have the broken heart, or will you? I'm talking about our cover story, of course,'' she said.

"You'll leave me with a broken heart,'' he replied. His voice sounded deeper than usual. "This is crazy...planning pretend weddings and plotting heartache. I should have told Millicent to mind her own damned business.''

Allison remained silent, wondering if Jesse was embarrassed by the whole thing. Due to circumstances beyond his control, he'd been handed a blind woman to protect. The cover story that she was a girlfriend come to visit had snowballed and now he found himself, in the eyes of the town, engaged to a helpless blind woman with a wedding less than seven weeks away.

"Jesse, when I leave here and things go back to normal, you can tell people the truth. You don't have to pretend to be nursing a broken heart,'' she said, wishing for the hundredth time she could see him and watch the emotions play in his eyes. It was so difficult to read people when you only had their voice, their words to go by.

"We'll see," he answered without commitment. "You ready to go?"

"Yes." She wiped her mouth with her napkin, then stood, waiting for Jesse to join her and guide her from the café. For some reason, the brief talk about her leaving here, leaving him with a broken heart, had depressed her. Silly, because she knew it was all just pretend.

"Tired?" he asked when they were back in his car and headed for his home.

"A little," she replied.

"If you don't mind, I want to swing by my office and grab a couple of files."

"Do whatever you need to do. I'm just along for the ride." She leaned her head back against the seat. The car not only retained the new smell, but also held Jesse's scent.

Masculine...slightly spicy, it was a fragrance that stirred a crazy yearning inside her, a yearning to feel his arms around her, to feel his breath against her face, to touch the muscled chest that she'd touched only hours ago.

Funny, her mother had taught her to be independent, but she'd never told Allison how to cope with the loneliness that self-reliance brought with it.

She fought against the desire to have Jesse hold her and instead opened her window a couple of inches, allowing in the summer night air laden with

the scent of flowers, and a faint whisper of hay.
The only sound she could hear was the singing of
the tires on the road.

The scents and lack of any other noise only
served to remind her of how far away from home
she was. Her Camelot was a place with sirens
screaming, horns blaring, people yelling—a ca-
cophony of noise that imbued the city with an underlying excitement and life.

Her Camelot was a single-bedroom apartment
decorated in her favorite styles and soothing colors,
a place too quiet, too lonely.

She frowned. Funny, she'd never thought of herself as lonely before. But now, as she remembered
how often she'd left her apartment to visit with Alicia and John, she realized there had been a deep
core of loneliness inside her for a very long time.

She pulled herself from her disturbing thoughts.
She was just lonely because she was out of her
element, away from her home and work. As soon
as she got her sight back and could return to Chicago, these strange thoughts and feelings would go
away. She straightened in the seat as the car came
to a stop.

"You can come in with me," Jesse said as he
shut off the engine. "You didn't officially meet Vic
this morning, and a couple of the other deputies
should be inside."

"All right," she agreed. Her hand smoothed her
hair self-consciously and before Jesse could get out
of the car, she touched his arm lightly, a blush

warming her cheeks. "I don't have mashed potatoes on my nose or anything like that, do I?"

For a moment the air was still, thick between them, as he leaned forward, so close she could feel his breath on her face. He touched the end of her nose, then trailed a finger down her cheek. "Nope, no errant mashed potatoes anywhere in sight." His voice was a low whisper that evoked heat to rise and rush through her.

He sat back abruptly and she heard his door open, then close. She drew in a trembling breath, wondering if he had any idea how the simplest touch from him affected her? She desperately hoped not.

By the time he opened the door to help her out of the car, the momentary flush of heat inside her had ebbed away. She tried to numb herself from the warmth of his hand on her elbow as he led her into the sheriff's office.

Their arrival was greeted by voices coming from all sides, momentarily disorienting Allison. She grabbed Jesse's arm for reassurance.

"Listen up, gang," Jesse said, his voice ringing with an authority Allison hadn't heard before. "I'd like you all to meet Cecilia Webster. Cecilia, to our immediate left is Rita Smith, my favorite dispatcher."

"Your only dispatcher," a robust female voice replied. "It's nice to meet you, Cecilia."

"And directly ahead of us is one of my deputies, Sam Black," Jesse continued.

"Howdy, ma'am." Sam's voice wasn't as deep as Jesse's, but was a nice mellow baritone.

"And seated at my desk, eating a piece of pizza that I'm sure isn't on his diet, is my right-hand man, Vic Taylor."

"It's just one piece, and I'm getting up from your desk right now." Allison recognized the deep voice from earlier in the day.

"Nice to meet you all," Allison said, "and please call me Cecilia." She released her hold on Jesse, feeling more secure now that she knew the occupants of the room.

"I hear wedding bells are going to be ringing soon," Rita said. "September is a nice month for a wedding."

"Jesse told me news travels fast in Mustang!" Allison exclaimed in astonishment. "We just set the date a little while ago."

"The *Mustang Monitor*'s office is right next door," Jesse explained.

"And Millie the motormouth stopped in a few minutes ago to fill us all in on the latest gossip," Sam said.

"Oh, I guess I didn't mention that Cecilia is Millicent's niece." Jesse's words were met with a stunned silence.

He laughed, the rich sound evoking a mesmerizing heat inside Allison. If he was even half as attractive as his laugh, then he was wonderfully handsome. "Got ya," he said to the silent, stunned group.

They all laughed as Sam good-naturedly cussed

his boss. When the laughter died down, the conversation quickly turned to something far more sobering.

"So, what do you think about Maggie?" Sam asked. "Do we have a copycat or has this creep gone over the edge?"

"It's too early to tell. We need more information," Jesse replied.

"I vote it's a copycat," Vic said. "Damn the newspaper for printing so much information about the first two crimes."

"Yeah," Sam agreed. "They practically gave everyone in town a blueprint to follow."

"Maybe, but we've got a lot of work ahead of us before we know for sure whether Casanova is now posing a new threat, or if we have another person victimizing the women of our town," Jesse said. "We know the crimes take place between the hours of midnight and four a.m. Starting tonight, I want a squad car to drive by the kissing tree at least twice an hour throughout the night."

"Bill and I can take turns doing drive-bys," Sam said.

"I'd like everyone to be here in the morning at seven-thirty. We'll go over everything then. Rita, see if you can get hold of Shelly and ask her to try to get to my house by seven in the morning," Jesse said and touched Allison's shoulder. "I'm finished here. Let's go home."

Allison nodded and stood. "It was a pleasure meeting you all," she said.

A few minutes later they were back in the car

heading home. Allison felt the weight of the day on her shoulders and knew Jesse's burden must be ten-fold. This was his town, his people, and he surely felt as if he had sole responsibility for solving these crimes.

"I wish there was something I could do to help," she said softly.

"At the moment there's not much anybody can do," he replied. "I need to go back and reinterview the first two victims, check the backgrounds of all of them, see if I can find a common thread." His voice held a wealth of frustration.

"Maybe with your men driving by the kissing tree regularly, it will prevent any more crimes," Allison observed.

"My biggest fear is that it won't prevent more crimes, it will just force the perpetrator to find a new location."

"What's your gut instinct? The same man or a copycat?" Allison asked.

"My gut instinct is that I'll probably have ulcers before this is all over." He sighed, a deep exhalation of breath like the forlorn winter wind that blew across Lake Michigan.

Allison fought the impulse to lean over, curl her arms around his neck and offer him comfort. She couldn't help him read files, she couldn't help him to look at crime-scene photos to see if she might spot something that had been overlooked. He was protecting her very life, providing sanctuary for her and she had little or nothing to give him back.

"We're home." He shut off the engine, but made

no move to get out of the car. Again he released a deep sigh. "Beginning tomorrow, while I'm at work, I'll have a deputy assigned to stay with you at the house," he said.

"Oh, no, Jesse. You can't do that," she insisted.

"Yes I can."

"But that isn't necessary," she protested. "Surely you need all your manpower to work the Casanova case. I'll be fine in the house alone. I don't want to be a burden to anyone."

"You're blind, Cecilia," he said the words flatly, but they struck her with the force of a pointed jab. "I need to have my attention solely on the Casanova case." He sounded angry. "Don't give me a hard time about this. What I don't need is to be at work trying to deal with Casanova yet worrying about you. Beginning tomorrow, there will be a deputy with you when I'm not home. And that's the end of this discussion."

He got out of the car and slammed the door. Allison opened the passenger door, but waited for him to escort her into the house, wishing with all her heart she could make it inside on her own.

But he'd been very clear in reminding her of her limitations. And in his angry words, she'd also been reminded of the fact that she was nothing more to him than a responsibility he was forced to handle. She would do well to remember that.

"Come on, Jesse. We'd better get home," Paul said worriedly. "It's getting late and the weather is supposed to get bad."

"In just a little while we'll go," Jesse replied, yelling to be heard above the din of the music. It was the best party he'd been to all year.

Suddenly, the scene changed. The party was gone, the music silent and Jesse and Paul were in Jesse's dad's car driving home. Paul had been right. They should have left the party earlier. Ice pellets bounced against their car window as they drove the isolated two-lane road home.

Jesse knew he was dreaming, and he fought against the continuation of the nightmare, wanting—needing—to awaken before the horrifying ending. And in his dream, the road gleamed black with ice, and he saw the tree in the distance...a twisted, gnarled tree that drew closer...closer...

He sat up with a strangled gasp, his heart racing, his body covered in a sheen of light perspiration.

He released a ragged breath of relief as he recognized that he'd left his dreamscape behind and was not in the car careening toward disaster, but rather in the comfort and safety of his own room.

Knowing from past experience that sleep remained elusive after one of these nightmares, he got out of bed and pulled on a pair of jeans. He turned on his bedside lamp, grabbed the files he'd brought home from the office, then left the bedroom.

As he walked past Cecilia's closed door, a trace of guilt swept through him. He'd hurt her feelings in the car. He'd taken the day's frustrations and vented them on her. Still, he wasn't about to leave her home alone, especially with the new development in the Casanova case. He'd told her the truth;

he couldn't afford to leave her on her own and worry about her.

In the kitchen he turned on the light, grabbed a soda, then settled himself at the table with some case files. He popped the top of the drink and took a long swallow, waiting for his heartbeat to resume a more normal pace.

He hadn't had that nightmare in years, thought he'd finally put the past far behind him. But Cecilia's blindness had brought it all back to him—the pain…and the guilt.

Not guilt, he protested. He had nothing to feel guilty about. It had been an accident, a tragic misfortune of fate. A little voice niggled in his mind. *You ran away. You ran as far and as fast as you could from Paul when you realized he was blind for life. You were a coward who couldn't handle his pain.*

"No," the single-word protest whispered from him. No, he hadn't run. He'd moved on to make things easier for Paul, afraid that his continued presence in Paul's life would make things more difficult for his best friend. It had been the right thing to do.

Jesse raked his hand through his hair and opened the first file in front of him and focused on the information contained within.

He didn't know how long he'd been at it when a noise roused him from his work. He looked up to see Cecilia in the doorway.

"Jesse?"

"Yeah, I'm here at the table," he said. She looked as beautiful as she'd looked that morning when she'd shared the tragic circumstances that had brought her here. Clad in sky-blue nightgown and robe, with her hair slightly tousled, she looked charmingly vulnerable, achingly touchable.

"Couldn't sleep?" she asked as she sat down across from him. He could smell summer flowers and he noticed how the blue of her nightclothes intensified the verdant shade of her eyes.

"Too much on my mind," he replied, and looked down at the files spread out across the table.

"What time is it?" she asked.

Jesse looked at the clock on the oven. "Almost one. What are you doing awake?"

She shrugged, the movement causing her robe to gap open enough for him to see her delicate collarbone and an expanse of creamy skin.

Desire hit him like a sizzling lightning bolt through his center. His heart boomed with the force of a hundred claps of thunder as he fought against the storm of wanting.

"What are you doing?" she asked.

Again he averted his gaze from her. "I've been looking over the reports, trying to find something, anything that might point to who is committing these Casanova crimes."

"Have you found anything?"

"No. I think I'm too tired to think." He hesitated a moment. "I'm sorry if I was brusque before...in the car."

She waved her hand to dismiss his apology. "Please, don't apologize. You have a crime to solve, and the last thing I want to do is get in your way. If you can do your job better by having a deputy stay with me, then so be it.''

"Thanks for understanding," he said. He studied her for a long moment. "What's it like...to be blind?" He didn't know he was going to ask the question, but once it left his lips, he realized it was something he wanted—needed—to know.

"I don't think it's something that can be explained. It has to be experienced," she said. "Turn out the light."

Jesse hesitated, already regretting the impulsive question, a question he knew was partially provoked by the nightmare he'd suffered earlier and thoughts of the man who had once been his friend.

"What's wrong, Sheriff? Afraid of the dark?" she asked, her voice holding a faint taunt.

"Of course not," he replied tersely. He stood and walked to the light switch on the wall. He turned it off, banishing the light from the room. It took only a moment for his eyes to adjust to the darkness.

"Tell me what you see." Her voice was soft.

"I see shadows...illumination around the window, moonbeams on the wall."

"Then you aren't blind yet."

He saw her rise from the table and approach where he stood. She passed through a silvery stream of moonlight, and Jesse's heart quickened at her beauty. The air seemed to thicken, making it more difficult for him to breathe.

She stopped when she stood mere inches from him and held out her hand. "Come with me."

Curious, he placed his hand in hers and allowed

her to lead him through the living room, down the hallway and into her bedroom. Jesse's heart hammered more rapidly in his chest. What was she doing?

As she opened the closet, he realized exactly what she intended. "Welcome to my world," she said as she pulled him into the small confines and shut the door.

Inside, the darkness was complete. There were no shadows, no break at all in the blackness that surrounded him.

"Let's sit," she said, and tugged him down to the floor of the closet. He sat with his back against the wall and his knees drawn up toward his chest. The feel of her body pressed against his side and her sweet fragrance enveloped him.

This isn't so bad, he thought. The dark wasn't as threatening as he'd imagined it might be. In fact, there was something oddly peaceful about it.

She shifted positions so that he had no physical contact with her whatsoever. In a single instant the darkness became disorienting, deeper and more profound. The momentary sense of peace fled and Jesse felt as if he'd been swallowed into the hole where loneliness abided.

Panic welled up inside him, a panic he'd never experienced before. Just as he was about to jump up and open the closet door, seek some kind of light to banish the darkness, her hand found his again and the anxiety ebbed.

"I can't tell you what everyone else's experience is like," she explained. "I can only tell you what mine has been like. At first it was so scary. Sometimes it still is.''

''At first it wasn't so bad, but then it made me feel very alone.''

''Exactly.'' She squeezed his hand more tightly. ''But it isn't all bad.''

''What's good about it?'' Jesse asked, now unable to imagine anything positive about being blind.

She released his hand once again, but her body relaxed against his side, warming him and keeping that momentary sense of utter isolation away.

''There's a certain peace contained in the darkness. Without the detraction of anything visual, it gives me more opportunity to think, to assess. Concentration is easier, and awareness is more acute. I can focus on a single sensory detail and not be distracted by anything else.''

Jesse knew exactly what she was talking about. Without vision, he was intensely aware of her softness next to him, her scent bewitching him.

Without visual input, his mind was free to create its own images, and the image that kept returning again and again in his mind was of her, dark hair in disarray, eyes an inviting green that enhanced the whisper-soft silk caressing her curves.

The darkness they shared in the closet evoked a compelling intimacy between them, and for just a brief moment Jesse wanted to tell her about Paul, and the accident, and the heartache that still had the capacity to haunt him.

He fought the impulse and instead rose to his feet in the small enclosure. ''It's late. We should be in

bed.'' The simple statement suddenly took on the
color of a double entendre and his cheeks warmed
in response.

He opened the closet door, then reached back in
for her hand and pulled her up. She rose far too
close to him and before he had time to think, before
he could stop his crazy impulse, he pressed his
mouth to the sweet curve of hers.

Chapter 6

The kiss caught her by surprise, but only momentarily. As Jesse's lips plied hers with fiery intent, Allison realized how much she'd wanted his kiss.

She wound her arms around his neck and opened her mouth to him, touching his tongue with the tip of hers. Her fingers splayed at the nape of his neck, reveling in the feel of his soft, thick hair.

He groaned and deepened the kiss as his arms pulled her tight against him. He drank of her, evoking a spark of desire deep within her as his hands stroked up her back, then down to her waist.

For the past month, Allison had felt lost in the dark, but Jesse's kiss, the warmth of his arms around her, the strength of his body so close to hers, provided a beacon of light that danced in her heart.

With an abruptness that stole her breath and

doused that momentary light, he broke the kiss and stepped back, breaking all physical contact between them.

"I'm sorry. That was stupid of me. I'm usually smart enough not to mix business and pleasure," he said, his voice brusque and deep.

"Don't worry about it," she replied, wondering how it was possible for the darkness of her world to grow deeper, more profound. "Let's just say the circumstances of too little sleep and too much night got the best of us."

"Good. I'm glad you understand. I'll just say good-night."

She knew the instant he left the room, felt his overwhelming presence gone from the air.

For a moment she remained absolutely still, her lips still retaining the heat, the imprint of his. The kiss had stolen her breath away. Even now, breathing was more difficult than it had been before his mouth had claimed hers.

Finally she took off her robe and climbed back into bed.

She didn't understand why he'd kissed her at all, but more, she didn't understand why his kiss had rocked her so thoroughly. It wasn't as if she'd never been kissed before.

She'd been involved in an intimate relationship once, several years ago. His name was Roger and he'd been her very first client.

She'd redecorated his apartment and they'd started dating. Within months, he was telling her he loved her, then trying to change everything about her. Their relationship had lasted six months. She'd realized he was more into control than love.

Still, none of Roger's kisses had moved her as quickly, as easily as Jesse's had. Her lips still burned with the memory of his touch.

He could have taken her to the bed and made love to her and she wouldn't have uttered a single word of protest. In fact, she would have encouraged him to make love to her, encouraged him to touch her, kiss her, meld with her.

And then what? She rolled over onto her back and stared blankly upward. He was a confirmed bachelor and professed to have no use for a wife or a family.

She was a woman in personal crisis, waiting to regain a life she had loved. This time in Mustang, this time with Jesse was a mere interlude, a forced intermission in her life. And when the intermission was over and the movie began again, she would be back in Chicago, back in her Camelot.

She cursed her sightless eyes. When would the darkness lift? The doctor had told her that if her sight was to return at all, it would return when she felt safe and secure. What if they never arrested John and Alicia's killers? What if she had to look over her shoulder for the rest of her life? Did that mean that she would never regain her sight?

She fought against a rising sense of panic. She was safe for now, here with Jesse, and at any moment she could open her eyes and find that her vision had returned.

What she couldn't do was allow herself to do

something stupid, something crazy with Jesse. She didn't want to find herself with her sight restored, only to discover that her heart had been broken.

Shoving away thoughts of Jesse, of her blindness and of her circumstances, she drifted into a deep, dreamless sleep.

When she awakened, she instantly realized it must be later in the day than when she usually woke up. The sunbeams she felt dancing through the window held the warmth of late morning. She dressed quickly, raked a brush through her hair, then dashed into the bathroom to wash her face and brush her teeth.

"Jesse?" she called moments later as she walked down the hallway to the living room.

"He's not here," a perky female voice replied from the direction of the sofa. "He left earlier for work."

"You must be Shelly," Allison said.

"That's right. Deputy Shelly Wattsman. And you're Cecilia, the lucky woman who captured our elusive sheriff's heart. I've got coffee on in the kitchen. Want a cup?"

"Sounds good," Allison agreed. Together the two women went into the kitchen. Allison took her usual place at the table and murmured her thanks as Shelly set a cup of coffee in front of her.

"I'm sorry you find yourself stuck with baby-sitting duty," Allison said apologetically when she knew Shelly had joined her at the table.

"Don't sweat it," Shelly replied with a light,

friendly tone. "So, you want me to tell you what I look like?"

"Okay," Allison replied with surprise.

"I have long blond hair and blue eyes. I'm five foot ten and weigh one hundred and fifteen pounds. Most of that weight is in my large, perfectly formed breasts." She paused a moment, then laughed. "Of course, you know I'm lying through my teeth."

Allison laughed, as well, instinctively knowing she was going to like Shelly. "Of course."

"Actually, I have naturally curly brown hair that I hate and brown eyes. I'm five foot four, weigh a hundred and forty pounds, and most of that weight I carry in my butt."

"It's nice to meet you, Shelly," Allison replied.

"Same here. So, tell me what you think of our little town."

Allison took a sip of her coffee, then replied. "Of course I can't comment on the beauty of Mustang, although Jesse assures me it's a picturesque little town. I can tell you the people I've met have been very kind."

"I was born and raised here and have never considered living anywhere else. Nonetheless, people coming here from a bigger city probably experience culture shock. They've probably never had the experience of living in a town where, if you belch, within minutes everyone knows about it."

Allison laughed. The humor felt good, banishing a strange, lingering melancholy from the events of the night before. Not the events, she mentally corrected herself. It had been a single event—Jesse's kiss and the knowledge that to repeat the pleasure would be utterly foolish—that had created the melancholy.

"Jesse told me you were a huge help yesterday with Maggie," Shelly said.

Allison shrugged. "I did what anyone would do. I offered her support."

"Poor Maggie."

"What do you think? One man, or was Maggie's assailant a copycat?"

"Who knows? Sad state of affairs in any case. Hard to believe one of our own is committing these crimes. Whoever it is, eventually we'll catch the creep. We might be a small town, but we have a good team of law enforcers."

"Tell me about the deputies," Allison said, enjoying the conversation and Shelly's friendliness, after having spent so much time alone and isolated.

"Well, there's Burt Ramsey. He's about forty-five years old, married and has two kids. A laid-back, nice guy. Then there's Vic Taylor. Vic is a big overstuffed teddy bear. He's always dieting and constantly trying to find a girl who'll take him seriously. Then there's Sam Black." Shelly paused, and Allison heard her take a sip of her coffee.

"Sam is handsome as sin, a real ladies' man and so full of himself, he makes me sick."

Despite the words spoken, Allison heard something telling in Shelly's voice. "You like him," she observed.

There was a long pause, then Shelly sighed. "I'm

crazy about the lug, but there's no way I'll give him the satisfaction of knowing that.''

"What about Jesse? How long have you known him?'' Allison knew she was foolish to ask questions about a man who was merely a temporary fixture in her life. But with the memory of his kiss on her lips, she found herself wanting to know him from another's perspective.

"Jesse and I went through school together.''

"Is he nice looking?'' Allison felt her cheeks warming with a blush.

Shelly laughed. "Yeah, Jesse is handsome, although personally, I like blond men. He was a real ladies' man in high school before the accident. His whole personality changed after that.''

"The accident?'' Allison leaned forward.

"The car accident. Hasn't he told you about it?''

"Maybe...I just don't remember,'' Allison hedged.

"If he told you, I think you definitely would have remembered. It was pretty traumatic.''

"You tell me.'' Allison forced a small smile. "You know how reticent men can be when it comes to sharing little pieces of themselves.''

"We were juniors in high school and Susan Maxwell had a big party. All the popular kids were invited. I wasn't, but I heard about the accident the next day at school. Jesse and Paul went to the party, and while they were driving home the weather got really nasty.''

"Paul?'' Allison interrupted her.

"Yeah, Paul Burke. He and Jesse were best

friends. Paul was sort of the golden boy at school. He was good-looking, played varsity football and there was talk about big scholarships coming his way."

"And there was an accident as they were driving home from the party," Allison said, stating the obvious.

"Yeah, a bad one. They hit a tree. Jesse wasn't seriously hurt, but Paul went through the windshield. I guess the glass cut up his face pretty badly and he wound up blind."

Blind. Suddenly Allison realized what had prompted Jesse's curiosity about what it was like to live in perpetual darkness. At the time he'd asked, a shiver of pleasure had washed through her. She'd thought he'd wanted to know what her world was like. But it hadn't been about her at all. "What happened afterward?" she asked.

"Paul was in the hospital for a while, then his family moved to Grange City, a little town about thirty miles from here."

"And what about Jesse?"

"Jesse changed after that night. It wasn't real obvious, but rather subtle. He was still friendly, still nice, but there was an aloofness about him, a remoteness that had never been there before."

"What about him and Paul?"

"Jesse never mentioned Paul's name again, and as far as anyone knows, they never got in touch after Paul moved. I think maybe Jesse couldn't handle Paul's blindness." She laughed self-consciously. "But I guess whatever hang-up he had about it, he got over it when he met you."

Maybe, Allison thought. But more likely, Jesse's agreement to protect her, his kindness, maybe even his kiss, were probably a result of him trying to deal with a trauma that hadn't been effectively dealt with in his past.

If she could see, if she was certain she could survive without help, she'd run now. She'd run away from the kiss that had awakened emotions inside her, emotions both thrilling and frightening.

She'd run away from the man who in the space of two single days had managed to make her realize the loneliness of the life she'd left behind.

And it was frighteningly impossible to guess what the future might hold for her.

She only knew one thing for certain. Somehow she would never be the same after her time spent with Sheriff Jesse Wilder in Mustang, Montana.

That damned kiss. Jesse sat at his desk, sipping coffee, but tasting Cecilia's sweet mouth. It was a kiss that never should have happened. He wasn't sure at this moment exactly how it had happened. One minute he'd been sitting in the dark in the closet, and the next he'd been kissing her.

Scowling, unsure whom he was more irritated with—Cecilia or himself—he focused his attention on the reports in front of him.

Three women... On the surface they were all apparently victims of Casanova. Jesse had gone to high school with all three of them, considered them friends and yet had no idea how to catch the man who had harmed them.

He hadn't been able to keep these women safe, and yet fate had handed him a blind woman with a gang of dirty cops after her. Could life get any more ironic?

He looked up as Vic entered the station carrying his lunch order along with Jesse's from the nearby café. He opened the foam container that held Jesse's hamburger and fries, then opened the second container to reveal a mountain of mashed potatoes smothered in creamy gravy and topped with a thick slab of country fried steak.

"Still on that diet, I see," he teased the big deputy.

Vic's face flushed a slight pink. "Go ahead, make fun. I admit it, I have no willpower, okay?" The edge in his voice surprised Jesse. Vic was always, unfailingly good-humored.

"I was just teasing you a little, Vic. What's up?"

Vic's flush deepened. "Sorry, I didn't mean to snap." He sat down in the chair across from Jesse's, a troubled frown furrowing his broad forehead. "And what's up is that I'm just sick about Maggie and what happened to her."

"We all are, Vic."

He nodded and they ate for a few minutes in silence.

"You know I dated her in high school," Vic said suddenly.

"Yeah, now that you mention it, I seem to remember the two of you dating for a while."

Vic nodded, his frown still cutting deeply into his brow. "She's always been real nice to me. It just kills me to think of her being hurt like that."

"You dated Kathy, too," Jesse said, and picked up the file on the first victim.

Vic nodded. "We were seniors. We only went out once. I also went out with Krista." Vic smiled sheepishly. "I think I dated every girl in the high school for at least one date." His smile widened. "At least you don't have to worry about dating ever again. Cecilia is real pretty and seems really nice. I just don't understand why you never told me about her before." There was a slight touch of hurt in the big man's voice.

Jesse frowned thoughtfully. He knew he'd be a fool to trust anyone, but between Cecilia and Casanova, he needed help. And if he couldn't trust Vic, a childhood friend and his deputy, who could he trust? "I probably shouldn't tell you this," he began, "but there might come a time in the next week or two that I need you to pull some extra hours. Between Cecilia and Casanova, I've got to make certain both bases are covered." He then went on to explain to Vic the real circumstances that had brought Cecilia to Mustang.

"So, you and her...you're not getting married?" Vic asked when Jesse had finished.

Jesse shook his head. "We hardly know each other. She's just here for her own safety and we figured it would be easier to explain her presence if we pretended to be involved."

"Poor pretty lady," Vic said softly.

"Yeah, she's had a rough time." He eyed his deputy sternly. "But you realize what I just told you about her is strictly confidential."

"'Course I do, Jesse. You know I'm not one to gossip none."

"And that's why I took you into my confidence," Jesse returned.

Vic nodded, obviously pleased by Jesse's show of trust, and again the two men resumed eating their lunches. As Jesse ate, he mentally chewed over the three cases.

Normally, in a case such as this, it is important to tie the victims together, to see at which places their lives meshed in order to find a perpetrator who would know all three.

In a town the size of Mustang, there were too many points where the women's lives would touch. They would have had their hair done at the same beauty shop, mailed packages at the same post office, bought groceries at the same store, had drinks at the same bar. And most likely, as single women, they had at one time or another all dated the same men.

"Wasn't Maggie dating some guy before this mess?" Jesse asked suddenly.

Vic nodded and paused a moment to swallow a mouthful of potatoes. "She was dating Burt Landry, a cowboy working for Cameron Gallagher, but I heard they quit seeing each other a couple of weeks ago."

Jesse stood and tossed his foam container into the nearby garbage can. "Maybe I should take a ride out to the Gallagher place and have a little chat with Landry, see what his alibis are for the nights in question.''

Vic's eyes lit up. ''You think he might be involved?''

Jesse shrugged. ''I don't know, Vic. Right now we're grasping at straws.'' He looked at his watch. ''I should be back in a couple of hours. Give Sam a call and have him meet us here at four o'clock.''

Minutes later, as Jesse left Mustang, he rolled down the window of his car to allow in the scents of late summer. Outside of the small town, the air was redolent with the smell of pastures and wildflowers, and somehow the scent reminded him of Cecilia. She always smelled of sweet, blooming flowers.

Damn that kiss. Damn her for molding herself so intimately against his body. Damn her for making him want her when they both knew there would never be anything long-term between them.

The last thing Jesse needed was a weeklong affair with a blind woman who would eventually get her sight back and return to her full, rich life in another state.

Jesse had managed to remain blissfully uninvolved with any woman for a very long time. When he'd become sheriff, he'd recognized the danger of dating any of the local women. He did not want his personal life picked and prodded, gossiped and chattered about among the people he served.

It was enough that he knew people were talking about him and Cecilia and their upcoming wedding.

Drat Millicent Creighton. Talking to her was sort of like dodging an oncoming train. Somehow she'd managed to maneuver Cecilia and Jesse into setting a wedding date when no wedding was intended.

He sighed as he pulled onto the Gallagher property. He'd face that particular mess when it happened. Despite his reluctance to the contrary, he'd play the role of brokenhearted lover for the people of Mustang when Cecilia left to return to her life.

He got out of his car, steadfastly shoving thoughts of Cecilia Webster aside. He had to stop thinking about her. He had more important things to focus on besides his desire for a woman who would be nothing but a distant memory within two more weeks or so.

It was after five when Jesse wearily walked up the steps to his porch. As he entered the house, he was surprised to smell something delicious in the air, something that smelled like roast.

Shelly must have cooked. He'd have to tell her that he didn't expect her to fix his evening meals while she was spending time here with Cecilia.

He walked through the living room and into the kitchen, surprised to see Shelly seated at the table and Cecilia standing next to the stove, stirring a saucepan of corn.

"Jesse?" Cecilia placed the spoon she'd been using on the counter and danced toward him.

Her face was glowing with a smile he'd not seen before. It lit her from within, removing the dark shadows of turmoil from her eyes and added a dash of bewitching color to her cheeks.

"I cooked." The two words sparkled in the air, shimmering in the wake of her enormous pride. "Shelly didn't help at all."

Jesse glanced at Shelly, who nodded her agreement. "She did it all, and I'm getting out of here," Shelly said, heading for the doorway. "Same time tomorrow, Jesse?"

He nodded absently and she gave a small wave, then disappeared from the kitchen.

"I did the entire meal all by myself."

For a moment Jesse didn't speak. He couldn't. Unexpected emotion reached out to clutch at him, making him momentarily speechless.

She looked so achingly beautiful, and the simplicity of her accomplishment and her pride therein touched him in places he'd never been touched before.

"Jesse?" Her brow creased with worry. "Is everything okay?"

"What could be wrong?" he replied. "Dinner smells wonderful."

"I cooked a roast and made a salad and heated up corn. I couldn't peel potatoes—I hope you don't mind doing without them."

"Potatoes. Who needs potatoes? I don't even like them that much," Jesse found himself saying.

Her brow smoothed and the beatific smile once again took reign over her features. "Good. Why don't you sit down and relax and I'll get the food on the table."

Jesse nodded, then remembered she couldn't see his nonverbal reply. "You want me to help?"

"No. I'd really like to do this on my own."

"Okay," he agreed, although a bit dubious as to how she would manage the serving process. He took his usual seat at the table and watched her work.

She worked methodically, her features set in deep concentration as she lifted the roast from the cooking pot and placed it on a serving platter. Carefully, easily maneuvering the kitchen space, she placed the platter on the table, then returned to the stove for the corn.

Within minutes she had everything on the table and she eased down in the chair opposite Jesse's, a smile of pride once again lighting her face.

"Does everything look all right?" she asked.

"It looks great." It was the truth. The roast looked juicy and cooked to perfection, the salad crisp and colorful with pieces of tomato and baby carrots, but Jesse was having difficulty focusing on the food.

Cecilia captured his full attention. Since the time she'd arrived, he'd seen her belligerent, filled with fear, angry and grieving. But until this moment, he'd never seen her with the light of sheer happiness shining from her eyes, her lips curved into a smile of pride and delight.

She was both beautiful and bewitching, and without warning his mouth tingled with the memory of the kiss they had shared.

He focused on the plate in front of him, realizing

he had to keep tight control over his emotions. If he didn't manage to remain both physically and emotionally untouched by her, he wouldn't have to pretend to have a broken heart when she finally left his home, his life.

Chapter 7

Allison had decided not to ask Jesse about Paul. She knew it was none of her business and that Jesse would probably only get angry with Shelly for talking too much about his personal life. And Allison had grown quite fond of Shelly.

For the past five days, Shelly had been at the house when Allison awoke. The two women had spent each day visiting with each other. Thankfully Shelly loved to talk.

She chatted about Mustang and the colorful characters that resided here, her lack of a love life, her crush on Sam Black, and her family, which included two brothers and two sisters.

Shelly didn't seem to notice that Allison shared very little of her own life, but Allison felt the stress of having to be careful of every word she spoke.

She never forgot that she was playing a role, the role of Jesse's loving fiancée.

Initially, Shelly's company reminded Allison of the times she'd spent with her sister. She and Alicia had often filled hours and hours with idle chat about fashion, men and marriage. Thoughts of Alicia and her husband brought with them a bittersweet pain.

It was stress that filled her as she left her bedroom early on Saturday morning and stumbled into the kitchen.

She'd awakened as always, with hope that when she opened her eyes, she would see the sun streaming through the window, see the room where she'd been sleeping for five nights. But the hope had lasted only as long as it took for her to open her eyes.

The moment she entered the kitchen, she knew it wasn't Shelly making coffee. "Jesse?"

"Yeah. How did you know it was me and not Shelly?" he asked.

"You smell different." She didn't elaborate, didn't want him to know that she found his clean, masculine scent wonderfully distinctive and enticing.

She sank down at the table. "Why are you home today? Did you break the Casanova case?"

"Not hardly. A cup of coffee is in front of you." He sat down across from her. "The Casanova case is going absolutely nowhere. No clues, no leads, nothing." His frustration was evident in his tone. "Oh, I almost forgot, I have a present for you."

"A present?" Allison's heart did a curious, wild leap. He'd bought her a present?

"Yeah, it's from Vic," he replied.

A wave of disappointment swept through her, instantly producing a renewed burst of irritation. Of course Jesse wouldn't have bought her a present. Why would he? She was nothing but an assignment to him.

He scooted back from the table and walked across the room. He returned a moment later and took his seat once again. "Hold out your hand," he instructed.

She did as he requested and a flash of awareness swept through her as he placed one of his hands beneath hers and with his other hand placed an object in her palm. He withdrew his hands immediately, taking the wave of heat with him.

Allison danced her fingers across the surface of the object. She knew it was soap, could smell the distinct minty scent she now realized she'd smelled both times she'd been around Vic. "It's a fish," she announced with delight as her mind worked to produce the image she held in her hand.

"Yeah. Vic carves bars of soap into different shapes. He's not bad at it, either. He mostly sells them at the county fair and at craft shows."

"How nice of him to think of me," she said, touched by the big deputy's thoughtfulness. She pushed the soap figure aside and grabbed her coffee cup once again, her earlier irritation returning as she thought of another day of being cooped up in the house.

"So, you think you might solve the Casanova case by staying home and baby-sitting me?" She knew her tone was peevish, but she couldn't help it.

"No, I don't think I'll solve it by baby-sitting you, but I did think perhaps a day off might give me some distance and objectivity." His tone was irritatingly patient.

He had been annoyingly polite to her since the night they'd shared the kiss. Actually, they'd had little time together alone since that night. Jesse had gone to work at the crack of dawn each morning and hadn't returned to the house until after eight each evening.

"Same jail, new jailer," Allison said, and took a sip of her coffee.

Jesse was silent for a long moment. "I didn't realize you felt as if you were in jail."

Allison sighed. "I feel as if I've been in jail since the night I saw Alicia's and John's murders. The cells change, the jailers change, but I'm still a prisoner." She offered him a small smile. "At least Shelly has been a more pleasant keeper than Kent Keller, who rarely uttered a single word."

Again Jesse was silent for a long moment. "Maybe we both could use a little break from the routine," he finally said. "Why don't we go camping? We could leave here in an hour or so and return before noon tomorrow when I should be back at the station."

"Are you serious?" The idea of leaving the house both thrilled and distressed her. She was tired of wandering the now familiar confines of the house and thought that a change of scenery, so to speak, would be exhilarating.

However, she was also aware that anywhere outside of this house she would once again be totally dependent on another person. Her sight limitations would be much more a hindrance once she left the structure of Jesse's house.

"I'm very serious." He scooted his chair away from the table and stood. "I think it's just what we both need. I always think better when I'm in the great outdoors, and you'll get a little vacation from your jail."

Allison could feel the energy that radiated from him.

"Are you game?"

"Sure," she agreed, a tiny thrill of adventure sweeping through her. "What do I need to do?"

"Sit here, finish your coffee, then get dressed. Jeans and a T-shirt, and you might bring a sweater or light jacket for the evening hours. I'll take care of the rest." With these words he disappeared from the kitchen.

Allison sipped her coffee and tried to imagine camping out. Did Jesse have a tent or would they sleep beneath the moon and stars? A moon and stars she wouldn't be able to see.

With a frown of irritation, she shoved this thought aside. She refused to let the day take on the dull gray of her blindness. She refused to allow self-pity to ruin a new adventure. A break in the routine would be good for her. With excitement winging through her, she finished her coffee, placed the cup in the dishwasher, then went to her room.

She placed the soap fish on her nightstand, again thinking how nice it had been of Vic to think of her. The soap sculpture would probably be the only souvenir she'd take back to Chicago with her when she left Mustang.

She quickly changed her clothes, her heart pumping with excitement as she thought of enjoying her first camping experience.

An hour later, she and Jesse were in his car. The back seat and trunk were packed with all the items Jesse said were necessary.

"Where are we going?" Allison asked when she sensed they'd left the city limits of Mustang.

"Whenever I don't have a lot of time but want to get away, I go to a national park about an hour from here. The camp sites are isolated but beautifully kept, and the scenery is breathtaking."

She sensed his wince. "If the scenery is beautiful, then it will be your job to describe it to me in glowing terms so I can see it in my mind."

"I've never been very good at painting pictures with words," he cautioned her.

She smiled. "Then you'll learn...just for me." She leaned back in the seat and felt herself relaxing. She could tell it was a beautiful day, could feel the strength of the sun against her arm and leg closest to the window.

"Did you camp as a boy?" she asked, curious about the man who seemed to occupy far too much of her thoughts.

"Just about every weekend when the weather was nice," he replied. "My dad was a real outdoorsman. He taught me a real love and respect for nature. He and my mom and me would pack up the car every Friday afternoon and camp until Sunday evening."

She could tell by the tone of his voice that those times were pleasant. She envied him his memories. She had so few good memories of her own childhood. There had been no time for fun in the Welch family.

"If somebody would have told me two months ago that I'd be in Montana and looking forward to camping for a night, I would have told them they were nuts," she said.

"I guess a big-city interior designer doesn't get much time to converse with nature." She heard the smile in his voice, and the desire to see his smile sent a sharp, deep ache through her. "So, what did you do in your free time for fun?"

"Oh, all kinds of things," she replied glibly, trying to remind herself of how much she'd loved her life in Chicago.

"Things like what?"

She frowned, trying to remember the life that, at the moment, seemed like somebody else's. "I took potential clients to dinner or sometimes to the theater."

"But that was basically work, right? Did you have hobbies of any kind? Things you liked to do when you weren't working?"

Her frown deepened. Hobbies? She'd never taken

the time to pursue any. She'd been taught that hobbies were a waste of time. "I mostly worked. I loved my work," she said with a forced passion. "And as soon as my sight returns, I'll get back to Chicago and continue doing what I love."

The vehemence of her answer seemed to take him aback. He fell silent, and so did she. The discussion had depressed her, and she wasn't sure why. All she knew for sure was that for the first time since arriving in Mustang, she wasn't particularly looking forward to returning home to Chicago.

Jesse wrestled with the tent, wondering if this hadn't been an enormous mistake. When he'd first suggested the camping trip, it had been an effort to break the monotony for Cecilia, but he had also hoped getting away from the confines of the house would alleviate the tension that had existed between them since the night they had kissed.

As he worked, he looked at Cecilia, who sat nearby on a dead, fallen tree trunk, her face lifted toward the sun. As if she sensed his gaze, she turned her head and offered a hesitant smile. "Are you sure there's nothing I can do to help?" she asked.

"No, thanks. I should have this thing set up in just a few minutes." He should have already had the tent erected, but his attention had been irritatingly distracted by her.

The sun fired rich red highlights in her dark hair and summoned a blush of color to her cheeks. With her face tilted upward, he found the smooth column of her neck inviting, the curve of her breasts against the thin cotton T-shirt enchanting and the length of her jean-clad legs fascinating.

So much for a change of venue easing the tension she managed to evoke in him, he thought. What on earth had he been thinking? He'd brought them from a house with many rooms to a tiny tent. Big mistake! He banged in a stake with more force than necessary.

Since the night of that damned kiss, Jesse had two things on his mind, two thoughts that were quickly approaching obsessive proportions. The first was catching Casanova. The second was making love to Cecilia.

The first was essential, the second was superfluous. Catching Casanova would be good for him, good for his town. Making love to Cecilia was fool's food, and Jesse was trying desperately not to taste the temptation.

"What do you do when you're camping out? I mean, besides sleeping in the tent."

"There are a couple of streams near here. Sometimes I do a little trout fishing, but I didn't bring the equipment today."

"You don't hunt, do you?"

He heard the underlying disapproval in her question and grinned. "No, I don't hunt, and I only catch the fish I intend to eat." He pounded in the last stake. "Most of the time when I come here, it's just to enjoy the quiet. I do a little hiking, sit and watch the sun set and listen to the nature that surrounds me."

Cecilia smiled. "After spending the last five days in Shelly's company, listening to nature will definitely be a change."

Jesse laughed. "Yeah, it will be much quieter. Shelly does like to talk, doesn't she?"

"She does, but she's very nice. Did you know she has a huge crush on Sam Black?"

"You're kidding." Surprise winged through Jesse as he thought of the two deputies. "Poor kid will probably have her heart broken. Sam isn't exactly commitment material."

Cecilia smiled. "You'd be surprised what love and a determined woman can accomplish." Her smile faltered slightly. "At least that's what I've heard, and that's what I want to believe."

There was a vulnerable wistfulness in her voice, as if she desperately wanted to find love, to be loved, but had so far found that particular emotion heartbreakingly elusive.

"Any special guy back in Chicago?" Jesse asked as he finished the last of the tent assembling. Surely a woman as beautiful, as sexy as Cecilia had a boyfriend.

She'd said she'd lost her family, but she hadn't mentioned a significant other in her conversation about her life in Chicago. How much easier it would make things for him if she had a boyfriend, somebody who owned her heart, and the kiss she'd shared with Jesse had simply been an anomaly brought on by her recent traumas.

"No, nobody special." Again he heard a wistfulness in her tone, a longing that was at once provocative. "I guess I never really took the time or trouble to pursue any kind of personal relationships."

"That's something you can change when you get back home," Jesse said. "I'm going to unload the rest of the things from the car," he said, his voice more gruff than usual.

Physical activity—that's what he needed. For some reason, Cecilia was getting beneath his skin and he found the itch she was creating in him distinctly uncomfortable.

"Want me to help?" she asked.

"No, thanks. I can get it," he replied, and stalked off toward the car parked in the distance.

It took him three trips from the car to the campsite to get everything set up to his satisfaction. By the time he was finished, the sun was high overhead and his stomach let him know it was lunchtime.

"Why don't we eat a sandwich, then take a hike?" he suggested.

"Sounds good," she agreed.

It took them only a few minutes to fix sandwiches from the cooler of food Jesse had brought along. As they ate, Jesse did his best to describe their immediate surroundings for her. As he did, he wondered who had described things to Paul over the years. Did he have a wife who acted as his eyes?

As always, thoughts of Paul brought with them the unsettling feeling of business unfinished, of loose ends that needed to be tied. As always, he consciously shoved uncomfortable thoughts of his old friend aside.

He was grateful when lunch was finished and they started on their hike. Jesse had always found hiking a mind-clearing activity; however, he'd never gone hiking with a desirable blind woman before.

He held Cecilia's hand as they walked down the well-worn trail, careful to watch for rocks that might trip her, or low-lying branches that might slap her.

If he'd been by himself, he would have chosen one of the less-traveled trails, but with Cecilia beside him he picked the widest, clearest path.

Their pace was snail slow and they'd only been walking a few minutes when Cecilia broke the silence between them. "Maybe it would be better if you took me back to the campsite." He heard a touch of frustration in her voice. "I could sit and wait while you do a little hiking."

He stopped walking and looked at her. "Do you want to go back?"

"Not really," she admitted. "But I'm forcing you to walk slow."

"I don't mind," he replied. "Besides, walking slowly, I'm seeing things I've never noticed before."

"Like what?" she asked as they continued on.

"I've never noticed before that there are wild-flowers all along here."

"What color are they?"

"White." He stopped and reached over along the

side of the path and picked one of the flowers. He took her hand and placed the flower gently in her palm.

She took the flower and twirled it between two fingers, then ran it along her cheek, as if enjoying the contact of soft petals against her skin. To Jesse, the simple act was rife with sensuality and a whirling heat spun to life in the pit of his stomach.

She brought the flower up beneath her nose and smiled. "It smells so pretty." She tucked the flower behind her ear, where the white petals were perfectly displayed against her dark strands of hair.

As they continued on, Jesse fought his growing awareness of her. The softness of her hand enticed him at the same time the distinctive scent of her seemed to surround him. Occasionally she bumped into him, and as her body touched his, tiny pinpoints of electricity ignited at each point of contact.

Jesse picked up their pace, wishing he could jog, run like the wind to escape the desire that burned in him. He'd been fighting it all week long. He'd hoped that getting them out of the confines of the house would ease the sexual tension he felt whenever she was near.

"Jesse, could we slow down just a little?" she asked after a few minutes.

He stopped and looked at her, saw the slightly panicked expression on her face, the fresh welt on her arm where a branch had apparently hit her, and cursed himself.

"I'm sorry," he said, and touched her arm where the skin was raised and red. He should be bullwhipped for careening down the trail without thought for her.

"It's all right. It's just a little frightening to move so fast when you're blind." Her chest rose and fell rapidly, and he didn't know if it was because of the pace they'd been keeping, or because his fingers still caressed the soft skin on her arm.

He dropped his hand, the pads of his fingers tingling from the momentary contact. "There's a little stream up ahead with a big, flat rock just perfect for sitting. We'll rest there for a few minutes."

"Okay," she agreed, a slight flush coloring her cheeks.

It took them only a few minutes to reach the rock that jutted out from the bank of the small, racing stream. The rock was big enough so they could sit and not touch, and that was just fine with Jesse.

They sat side by side, their legs stretched out before them. Although the rock was now shaded by the branches of a nearby tree, it still retained the heat of the sun from earlier in the day.

The stream gurgled and splashed, creating a pleasant natural music. Overhead, a bird whistled a sweet song and the leaves of the trees whispered as a breeze blew through them.

Slowly Jesse felt himself relaxing. He'd spent many hours over the years on this very rock, seeking the kind of peace and tranquillity only isolation and Mother Nature could offer.

"It's beautiful here, isn't it?" Cecilia's voice was soft, as if in reverence of their surroundings.

"Yes, it is," he agreed.

She nodded. "It sounds beautiful."

"I wish you could see it…the way the water trips over the rocks, and when the sun shines just so, it turns the water silvery. Every once in a while you can see a fish break the surface and make rings."

Jesse paused a moment, then continued. "There is a small clearing on the other side of the stream and it looks like it's a place where deer and other wildlife come down to the water to drink. There's also a patch of those wildflowers just downstream from where we're sitting."

Cecilia smiled and covered his hand with hers. "Thank you," she said simply.

"For what?" He wondered if she had any idea what her slightest touch did to him, if she was aware of the fires she ignited each time their flesh met in any way.

"For helping me see." She took her hand from his, allowing him to breathe again.

"That's funny, I was just thinking the same thing," he replied.

"What do you mean?" Her eyes were the green of the nearby trees.

"In describing it all to you, it was like I was seeing it for the first time." It was true, he thought in surprise. She was the blind one, but she was helping him see.

"It's funny." She pulled her knees up to her chest and wrapped her arms around them, her expression contemplative. "Right here, right now, I don't feel quite so blind. My other senses are so full of impressions, and thanks to you, I have a clear mental picture of the surroundings.''

"This is one of my most favorite places in thc whole world," Jesse said. "I've spent a lot of time over the years right here on this rock, contemplating life's problems and mysteries. Somehow, sitting here in the middle of nature made those problems and mysteries a little less daunting.''

Cecilia reached out her hand and placed it on his arm. "Thank you, Jesse.''

"For what?''

"For bringing me camping, for sharing your favorite place with me. But most of all, for making me feel completely safe whenever I'm with you.''

Jesse wanted to protest. As he thought of the two of them, alone in the tent for the night, he knew this camping trip had been an enormous mistake. She wasn't safe. She especially wasn't safe from him.

Chapter 8

"This is absolutely the best meal I've ever had," Allison said as she ate the steak and baked potato Jesse had cooked over the flames of an open fire.

"It is good, isn't it?" Jesse agreed. "There's nothing better than food cooked over a fire."

"The whole afternoon has been wonderful." And it had been.

They had spent several hours sitting on the rock, sometimes talking about nothing important and other times merely enjoying a companionable silence.

On the way back, they had made a pit stop at the nearby public facilities, then returned to the campsite. Allison had sat on the fallen tree trunk while Jesse prepared dinner.

As he worked, Jesse had entertained her with stories about past camping experiences, displaying a delightful sense of humor that kept her laughing and protesting that he was making it all up.

She knew when evening was falling by the cooling temperature and was grateful when Jesse built a fire, which released plenty of smoke-fragrant heat.

Chicago and her previous life seemed far away as insects began their night songs, filling the air with their musical clicking and whirring. At the moment the world seemed to exist in sum and total of Jesse, herself and the approaching night.

She had been acutely conscious of Jesse throughout the course of the afternoon. His hand holding hers as they'd hiked had stirred a hunger inside her, a hunger she knew couldn't be satisfied with the steak he'd prepared.

She wanted to taste his kiss once again. It was a foolish desire and she knew it. What possible good could come of kissing Jesse? She had no intention of staying in Mustang. Besides, she didn't trust her own reasons for wanting Jesse.

Did she want him because she was falling for him? Or were her reasons more complex than that? He had come to represent safety to her, safety in a world that was frightening and fraught with danger and uncertainty.

Was she mistaking her gratitude for everything he was doing for her, for something more? Was she mistaking gratefulness for desire?

"Have you thought any more about the case?" she asked, eager to divert her attention from her own inner turmoil.

Jesse sighed, and in that sigh she heard his deep frustration. He sat next to her on the log. Although they were in no way touching, she felt as if he touched her with his very nearness. "Off and on throughout the day, but nothing is clear. What bothers me is that I know most of the people in Mustang, and I can't imagine any of them kidnapping or raping anyone."

"Is it possible Casanova is a drifter? Somebody who doesn't live in Mustang and maybe has moved on?"

"I wish, but I don't think so." Again he sighed, and Allison felt the desire to take him in her arms and hold him until his despair was gone. "This man seems to know too much about his victims...that they were single and lived alone."

"Tell me again all the details about the victims and the crimes. Maybe something will come to you as you repeat everything, or maybe I'll hear something that might help." She was anxious to keep her mind on anything other than Jesse and how much she'd like to lure him into their tent and make love with him.

"Are you sure you want to hear it?"

"Absolutely." She took the last bite of her steak, then placed her plate on the ground next to her feet.

As he spoke, telling her all of the details, Allison tried desperately to focus on his words.

Just for a moment she'd wished to see his face. She wanted to see the sparkle in his eyes, wanted to view the tiny lines that radiated out from them. She'd like to observe his expressions, and more than anything she wanted to behold the glory of his smile.

Perhaps fate was being kind by not allowing her to see him. This way when she returned to Chicago, she'd have no visual memories of him to torment her.

"At least with your deputies driving by the kissing tree at night, there haven't been any new incidences," she said when he'd finished.

"Yeah, but what worries me is that I believe it's just a matter of time before he figures out that deputies can't be at the tree all the time. I just don't have the manpower to keep the tree under surveillance twenty-four hours a day, and every night there are several windows of opportunity for this creep."

"You said the women were all about the same age. Could that be a clue?"

"Sure, although it could mean a number of things. It could be that the perpetrator, for some reason or another, is only interested in victims in that age range. It could mean the perpetrator himself is about that same age. It could mean a hundred different things, but it's not a clue that gives me much help."

"And he left no actual physical evidence behind."

"None. But if Casanova is the one who raped Maggie, then he might have made his first mistake. I know now that whoever raped Maggie has AB blood, and with DNA testing we can use that information to convict him. The only problem with that is we have to catch him first."

Allison reached out and found his hand on the log next to hers. She covered it with her own. "You'll get him, Jesse. I have all the faith in the world in you."

"Thanks for the vote of confidence. That and a dollar might get me a cup of coffee, but not much else," he replied, a touch of humor lightening his voice.

Allison released his hand, not because she wanted to, but because she didn't want to. Instead she held her hands out toward the warmth of the fire and for a few minutes they fell into an easy silence.

She could easily imagine the darkness of night closing in around them, the firelight casting deep shadows and providing an immediate circle of light that shone only on the two of them. There was something intimate in the setting.

There were no other people nearby, no watchful eyes, no gossiping tongues, and the knowledge that they were so utterly alone added to the aura of intimacy.

"What kind of a moon is out there tonight?" she asked.

"Almost full, but not quite," he replied.

"I must confess, I'm quite disappointed." She cast a teasing smile in his direction.

"Disappointed?"

"I thought here in Camelot the moon would always be a big, fat, full one."

He laughed, and the sound sent a ripple of heat through her. "Actually, Camelot enjoys a regular moon, with all its phases. A full moon every night would be boring.''

"And we can't have boring in Camelot, right?"

"Right," he agreed.

Again they fell quiet. The fire popped and crackled, a sound Allison found oddly pleasing. She drew in a deep breath, enjoying the scents of the night, the surrounding woods and the fire.

She was more relaxed than she could remember being in a long time. The day of simply enjoying nature had produced a sense of peace that had been sadly lacking for the past weeks.

"You know what I like about you?" Jesse asked suddenly.

She looked in his direction with surprise. "No, what?"

"You don't seem to feel the need to fill every silence with chatter. That's a nice quality to have."

"When you live a lonely life, you get used to the silence." She frowned. "I don't mean lonely, I mean I spend a lot of time alone."

A Freudian slip? With each day that passed she gained more objectivity about the life she'd left behind, and she realized that life had not been as wonderful as she'd once convinced herself it was. But, good or bad, it had been her life...a life snatched away by violence. Would she even get it back?

She released a deep sigh. "Every time the phone rings, I think it's going to be Kent Keller or Bob Sandford telling me they've caught the bad cops and I can go home."

"I'm sure you're anxious to get back."

"It's not that." She once again held her hands out toward the warmth of the fire. "I just keep thinking that when I know the guilty cops are behind bars, when I know none of them can get to me, then my sight will return."

"How do you know that? What if it doesn't?" His questions hung in the air, unwelcomed in the possibilities they yielded.

"It will." She said the words firmly, refusing to consider any other likelihood. Then, desperate to change the subject, she smiled. "So, now that we have all that out of the way, let's talk about what else you like about me besides my ability to appreciate silence."

He laughed and shifted positions and his thigh came to rest against hers. "Leave it to a woman to try to wheedle compliments from a man."

"Leave it to a man to force a woman to have to wheedle compliments from him," she countered. She wished he'd move his thigh, yet hoped longingly he wouldn't move.

There was a long pause. "I like the way your hair reflects the glow of the fire." His fingers lightly touched a strand of her hair, and she suppressed a shiver that threatened to race up her spine.

He cleared his throat and jumped up. "How about some dessert? I brought marshmallows to roast over the fire."

"Okay," she replied, disappointed that he'd distanced himself from her. "I don't think you want me with a stick around the fire. How about you roast them and I'll eat them?"

"It's a deal," he said.

Allison heard an underlying tension in his voice, a tension she felt in the very pit of her stomach. She could identify her own...desire. Was it possible he felt the same way?

The shiver she'd worked so hard to suppress broke free and shimmied up her spine as she thought of the two of them indulging their desire for each other.

"One marshmallow coming up," he said. "Are you ready?"

She could tell he was mere inches in front of her by the immediate nearness of his voice. "Ready," she replied.

"Open your mouth."

She did and he fed her the warm, sweet treat. As her tongue touched the tip of his finger, heat suffused her. He pulled his hand away as if she'd bitten him.

Again heat swept through her, along with a bit of elation. It wasn't just her. He felt it, too—the energy, the force of magnetism between them. She didn't just imagine it; it wasn't something she alone experienced.

"Could I have another one?" she asked.

"Sure." His single-syllable reply transmitted a wealth of tension and Allison reveled in it. He wanted her. She knew it and it filled her with the rush of luscious anticipation.

"Here you go." His voice was deeper, more husky than usual.

Allison opened her mouth, and at the same time

placed her hand over his so he couldn't withdraw from her before she was ready. He hissed inward as her tongue lathed his captured fingers.

"Cecilia, you're treading on dangerous ground," he finally said. The warning she heard in his tone thrilled her.

"Hmm, I hope so," she replied, then released his hand and stood, praying he would take her in his arms and kiss her until her head spun and her knees buckled.

To her dismay, he retreated. "I think it's time we call it a night," he said, and she could tell from the direction his voice came that he had moved to the opposite side of the fire from where she stood.

The anticipation, the thrill she'd felt only a second before seeped out of her. Had she mistaken his reaction? Damn her blindness.

It was so hard to figure out thoughts and feelings without being able to see a person's expressions. If she could look into his eyes, would she see the flames of desire...or mere indifference? Or worse, pity for the poor blind woman who had the hots for him.

Weariness replaced everything else. "Yes, yes, I'm tired," she agreed.

She jumped as his hand touched hers. She hadn't been aware of his approach. "Come on," he said. "I'll get you settled in, then I'll take care of banking the fire."

She nodded, allowing him to lead her, like he would a docile child, past the fire to where the tent stood. He released her hand only long enough to unzip the flap, then he helped her into the small confines.

He helped her locate her sleeping bag. "Will you be okay while I take care of the fire?" he asked.

"Of course," she replied. She heard him leave the tent and lower the flap behind him. For the first time since coming to Mustang, she felt utterly alone.

She climbed into the sleeping bag and instantly realized she'd be more comfortable if she'd take off her jeans. She kicked them off, folded them up, then placed them near her pillow where she could grab them first thing in the morning.

The ground beneath her was hard and uncomfortable, but no more uncomfortable than the ache in the pit of her stomach—an ache of unfulfillment.

What was wrong with her? What was it about Jesse that had her thinking such crazy thoughts?

She closed her eyes and drew a deep breath, trying to forget that the fire she really wanted Jesse to bank was right here in the tent.

Jesse stared at the dying embers, wishing the flames inside his gut would die the same sort of unremarkable death.

Cecilia had stirred a hunger in him of mammoth proportions, and he didn't quite know what to do about it. He wanted to be an honorable man. Her care and well-being had been entrusted to him. But the thoughts skittering through his head were distinctly dishonorable. Rather, they were wild, and hot and wonderful.

He kicked dirt over the last of the fire, then sank down on the log and stared up at the moon. He knew what he was doing—stalling...biding time...waiting to get his emotions under control before he climbed into that tent with Cecilia.

A wave of heat threatened to consume him as he thought of the way her mouth had felt wrapped warmly—wetly—around his finger. It had been the single, most sensual act Jesse had ever experienced, and it had nearly undone him.

He'd seen the passion in her eyes, felt her need for him, and he wasn't sure if he was a fool or a hero for reining her in, for detouring the situation out of the danger zone.

Would he be taking advantage of her if he made love to her? Granted, her personal life was in turmoil and she had suffered enormous losses. But he and Cecilia were both adults; they both knew the score.

It wasn't as if he'd be seducing her. Hell, if anything, he thought she might have been trying to seduce him.

He stood, tired of his thoughts, tired of the torment. She'd probably fallen asleep by now, any crazy moment of desire gone and forgotten. He lifted a kerosene lantern, checked the fire one last time, then headed for the tent, intent on going right to sleep.

The first thing he noticed when he entered the tent was her jeans neatly folded next to where she lay. Instantly his mind produced a picture of her long naked legs.

He tripped over his sleeping bag and muttered a low curse. This whole camping trip had been the worst idea he'd ever had. At least he was grateful she was turned away from him, her hair a dark spill against the red sleeping bag.

He sat down on his own bag and took off his boots, then shucked his jeans and T-shirt. He never slept in more than his briefs and he wasn't about to change his habits now.

He got into the sleeping bag and turned off the lantern, instantly plunging the interior of the tent into complete darkness.

It was difficult to tell if she was really sleeping or not. With her head turned away from him, he couldn't hear the rhythm of her breathing to know for sure.

Willing his body to relax, he drew in several deep breaths, wondering how it was possible for Cecilia's scent to overtake the entire space. The feminine, floral scent invaded his head and caused the coil of heat to return to his stomach.

He didn't know how long he lay there, thought he might have fallen asleep for a few minutes, when Cecilia started to moan. The moans were soft, but filled with anguish and he could hear her thrashing about in the confines of her sleeping bag.

She was having a nightmare. "Cecilia," he said. She didn't respond to him, but continued to moan in torment.

He sat up and lit the lantern, then leaned over her and grabbed her by the shoulders. "Cecilia, wake up," he said more sharply as he gave her a little shake.

Her eyes fluttered open, their green depths holding remnants of fear. "Jesse?" she whispered.

"You were having a nightmare," he explained.

"Yes, now I remember." Tears welled up in her eyes, a mist that made them all the more luminous. "I was so frightened, and so alone. Hold me, Jesse." She curled her arms around his neck. "Please hold me. I'm scared. I'm so scared of the dark."

He gathered her in his arms, secure in the fact that nothing would come from a comforting embrace. They were each in their own sleeping bag, mounds of material keeping the embrace from being too intimate.

She clung to him, her face buried in the hollow of his throat. Jesse was in complete control until she pressed her lips against his neck and that single, simple act made his control snap.

With fire in his veins, he took possession of her mouth, kissing her with the depth and desire he'd wanted to for the past week.

She returned the kiss with the same kind of ardor, her mouth opening to willingly invite him to explore. His hands tangled in her hair as her hands wandered the wide expanse of his back.

She tasted of marshmallows and desire, of honey and heat, a heady combination that sizzled through him. His tongue danced with hers, advancing then retreating, heightening the pleasure of the kiss.

He was lost in her and didn't want to be found.

The sleeping bags, that only moments before had been a measure of safety and security, now became nuisances, barriers that kept him from fully touching her.

When the kiss finally ended, her breathing matched his, ragged and uneven. He pulled away, some semblance of control returning. "Cecilia, this isn't a good idea."

"Why?" She sat up and shoved a strand of hair behind her ear. "I want you to hold me in your arms, make love to me. We're both adults. I'm not asking for you to kiss me beneath the kissing tree and make a forever vow. All I want is tonight." To punctuate her sentence, she pulled her T-shirt over her head and tossed it aside.

Jesse's breath caught in his throat as his gaze hungrily devoured the sight of her. The wispy, lacy bra did little to cover her breasts, and he could see her nipples, taut and pink beneath the filmy material. His response was immediate and visceral.

He unzipped his bag at the same time she kicked free of hers and suddenly they were skin against skin, bare legs tangling together as they deepened their kiss once again.

All thought of right or wrong was gone. This was right. Everything inside him told him making love to Cecilia at this moment in time was right.

"Do you have the lantern on?" she asked breathlessly.

"Yes." His reply was just as breathless.

"Please turn it off."

"But I want to see you," he protested.

"Then see me through touch, as I see you."

He hesitated only a moment, then did as she bid, plunging them into darkness. Again they found each other, needing no light to resume the heated caresses, the hungry kisses they craved.

Jesse's mouth left hers to trail down the side of her neck. She moaned, a deep, guttural sound that stirred him as his hands covered her breasts. He rubbed his fingers across her nipples, felt them pressing against the bra with urgency. She arched against him, emitting another deep moan, and Jesse felt as if he might explode.

Slow, he told himself. He wanted to go slow, to savor every taste, every sensation. He wanted to go slow and pleasure her as much as possible before reaching his own peak of pleasure.

He ran his hands down the flat of her stomach, pausing at the low waistband of her panties. She cried out in delight as he found the center of her heat, rubbing her through the thin, silky material. She moved her hips against him as her hand skimmed beneath his cotton briefs to stroke him.

Her intimate touch drove him wild and it seemed to do the same to her as she removed her panties, then helped him remove his briefs. With no barriers between them, they pressed their bodies together, hip to hip, thigh to thigh.

Suddenly slow no longer seemed an option. "Cecilia." He groaned her name as he rolled over on top of her and her legs parted to welcome him.

"Allison," she said breathlessly. "Please, call me Allison."

"Allison," he replied. Someplace in the back of his mind, he knew he shouldn't know her real name, but he understood her need to be herself, to hear her real name at this moment in time. "Sweet Allison," he whispered as he entered her.

"Oh, Jesse, love me," she whispered against his neck, her hands convulsively clutching at his back.

And he did. Initially he moved slowly against her, closing his eyes as her warmth enveloped him. He was lost in her—lost in her scent, her feel, the very essence of her.

It was she who quickened the pace, pulling him faster, deeper into her. As he possessed her, he found himself whispering her name over and over again, loving the sound of it in the air, the feel of it on his lips.

He had no idea what the next day would bring, wasn't even sure how great their regret would be. At the moment it didn't matter. Nothing mattered but the fact that he was lost in Allison, and that's exactly where he wanted to be.

Chapter 9

Allison knew without opening her eyes that dawn must be approaching. The insect noises that had served as a lullaby for most of the night had quieted and had been replaced by birdsong heralding the start of a new day.

Allison awakened to find herself intricately entwined with Jesse. Her head was on his chest, one leg wrapped with his. One of his arms was around her back and his hand rested on her bare hip. The intimacy of their naked embrace thrilled her.

She remained unmoving, wallowing in the sweet sensation of being held in his arms. She loved the feel of him, the smell of him.

She could feel the beat of his heart beneath her ear, the slow easy cadence of sleep. His skin was warm and the hair on his chest was soft beneath her cheek.

With her eyes still closed, her mind replayed every caress, each kiss they'd shared. Each glorious detail was burned into her mind.

Making love with Jesse had been more wonderful than she'd imagined. He'd been hungry and demanding, yet giving and patient at the same time.

She wondered if each caress, each stroke of his hands had been more intense because of her blindness, yet instantly discounted the theory. After all, when she'd been with Roger, they'd always made love in the dark, and she'd always kept her eyes closed.

No, the incredible intensity had sprung from something else, and she refused to delve too deeply into the reasons for it, afraid of what the answers might be. It was enough to say he'd made her feel things she'd never felt before, and she wondered how long it would take her to forget the experience once she returned to Chicago.

Perhaps given enough time she might forget the intensity of their lovemaking, but she had a feeling she would never be able to completely forget making love with Jesse. She would never be able to completely forget Jesse.

She frowned, wondering if everything her mother had ever told her was wrong. Was it so bad to need somebody? To want to belong to something bigger than just yourself?

Certainly Alicia had believed their mother was wrong. Despite the teachings of independence, she had built something beautiful with John, a symbiotic relationship based on weaknesses and strengths, desires and needs. What could be more right than that?

Jesse's heartbeat changed rhythms, gradually stepping up its pace as he came awake. She knew the moment total consciousness claimed him, for his heart thudded with a rapid fire beat that coursed through her, as well.

Apparently unaware that she was already awake, his hand lightly caressed her hip and thigh, as if loving the feel of her skin.

There was a part of her that wanted to continue to pretend slumber so he wouldn't stop, but another part of her recognized the danger of doing so. Did she want to create another memory that would haunt her for the rest of her life?

She stirred, as if just coming awake, then raised her head. "Good morning."

His hand stopped its movement and he instantly pulled it away from her. Allison felt both relief and disappointment. Simultaneously they sat up and un-tangled from each other so they weren't touching.

"You ready for some breakfast?" he asked. She could tell by where his voice came from that he had stood. She heard the whisper of material, then the rasp of his zipper being pulled up and knew he'd put on his jeans.

"No, I'm really not hungry." Her face flamed as she was once again reminded of her helpless dependence on him. "Jesse, could you find my clothes, please?"

She hadn't felt naked or vulnerable until now, knowing he was dressed and she had no clue where her clothes had been tossed during last night's escapade. It would take her forever to find them by rummaging around the confines of the tent.

"Sure." He found the items and placed them in her lap. "If you don't want breakfast, then maybe we'll just go ahead and load up and head back to town."

She nodded. "Just give me a couple of minutes to dress."

"I'll be outside." He unzipped the tent flap and stepped out, taking a palpable energy with him.

Allison breathed a sigh and hurriedly pulled on her panties, then donned her bra. Apparently Jesse didn't intend a Monday-morning quarterback kind of discussion about what they had shared the night before.

That was fine with her. After all, what was there to say about it? That it was good, wonderful even, and that it shouldn't happen again because nothing would come of it? She already knew all that so there was no point in hashing it out aloud.

Even if Allison allowed herself to think she might have a life in Mustang, that she could leave behind all she'd been building in Chicago, Jesse deserved better than a needy, blind woman in his life.

And when she regained her sight, would she still entertain the idea of making Mustang her home, or would she eagerly return to her shop and her life in Chicago?

Shoving aside thoughts of what if, she finished dressing and stepped out of the tent. The morning

smelled crisp and clean and Allison drew in a lung-
ful of the slightly pine, fresh air.

"It feels like it's a beautiful morning," she said,
gazing in the direction where she heard Jesse packing items.

"We'll have rain before nightfall," he said.
"There're already storm clouds gathering."

"I don't mind rain. In fact, I've always found it
rather soothing." She sat on the fallen log where
she'd spent much of the evening before. "I'm assuming the best thing I can do to help you is to
stay out of your way."

"Yeah, it won't take me long to knock down the
camp and we'll be on our way." She sensed tension
in his voice. For a few minutes he worked in silence. Allison wondered if he regretted last night.
What seemed like a good idea in the darkness of
night often became foolish with the illumination of
dawn's light.

Was he afraid that she might read more into it
than it had meant to him? Was he worried that
she'd suddenly demand more of him than he intended to give?

"Jesse, you don't have to worry, you know," she
said.

"Worry?" She heard the bewilderment in his
voice. "Worry about what?"

"That somehow I'll make more of last night than
it was, that I'll demand something of you that you
don't want to give." She forced a small laugh. "I
just want you to know you can relax. Last night
was wonderful, but we both know it was purely a

physical release of energy that had been building between us. We both know it didn't really mean anything.''

He was silent for a long moment and for the hundredth time she wished she could see his features, read his expression. ''Okay, then I won't worry,'' he said.

Again he worked in silence. She heard him take down the tent and fold it, box up the lanterns and roll up the sleeping bags.

''This trip didn't exactly accomplish what you hoped it would, did it?'' she asked as they walked toward the car to leave the campsite.

''You mean as far as the Casanova case?'' he asked.

''Yes.'' He opened her car door and she slid into the passenger seat.

He didn't answer her until he was seated in the driver side. ''No, I didn't suddenly solve the crimes or gain some meaningful insight, nor did I really expect that to happen.'' He started the engine with a roar. ''But I do feel like I'm going back with my head more clear.''

''Hopefully nothing happened last night while we were gone,'' Allison said.

It was as if her words had jinxed them. When they pulled into Jesse's driveway, Amanda Creighton was waiting for them on Jesse's front porch.

''What's going on, Amanda?'' Jesse asked as he helped Allison from the car.

''You need to talk to Maggie,'' Amanda said, her agitation apparent in the slightly shrill tone of her voice. "She's letting that damned Burt Landry move back in with her."

"I don't understand. What's the problem?" Jesse asked.

"The problem is Burt Landry is a creep and she broke up with him weeks ago. It was the smartest thing she's ever done. But her trauma has made her vulnerable and she's making a bad mistake by letting him back into her life."

"What am I supposed to do? Arrest her for showing bad judgment?" His voice was laced with dry humor. "If that's the case, I'd be arresting nearly everyone in town, including myself."

Amanda sighed in frustration. "Cecilia, will you talk to her?" Amanda grasped Allison's hands. "She trusts and admires you. Just make sure she has her head on straight, that she really knows what she's doing. Please. I don't want her hurt anymore."

"Okay," Jesse relented. "We'll take a ride over there and talk to her."

"Thank you." Amanda gave Allison's hands a squeeze, then released them. "I just hate to see her make a mistake because of what she's been through."

Minutes later, Jesse and Allison were back in the car, heading for Maggie's place. "I guess the sheriffs in small towns wear many hats," Allison said.

"I suppose we do," Jesse agreed. "Law enforcement, surrogate priest, sage adviser. I've even been known to don a coaching hat for the local Little League team."

"Tell me about Burt Landry. Why does Amanda think he's a creep?"

"Amanda thinks most of the men in Mustang are creeps," Jesse said, a light humor in his voice. "Amanda is waiting for a prince and all she keeps finding around here is cowboys."

"And she doesn't like cowboys?"

"Hates 'em. Anyway, Burt Landry is a swaggering, macho kind of cowboy. He drinks too much, talks too loud and usually most weekends finds himself in the middle of a brawl out at the Round-Up."

"Doesn't sound like my kind of hero," Allison said. "But that doesn't mean he can't be Maggie's kind of man."

"True," he said easily. "The only reason I agreed to drive over here and talk to Maggie is because I'm worried about her. Amanda's right. She's been through a terrible ordeal, and I don't want her making things worse on herself because she's not emotionally stable."

Allison reached over and touched his thigh. It was a light, momentary touch, but the contact sent heat rippling through her. "This town is lucky to have a sheriff like you."

"Yeah, we'll see if they still feel lucky if I don't catch Casanova." He slowed the car. "Amanda was right. Burt's old pickup is at Maggie's and it looks like he's moving in." He pulled the car to a stop. "I checked out Landry a couple of days ago, checked his alibis for the three nights in question. He had pretty solid alibis for all three nights."

"Then at least we know he's just your garden-variety creep and not anything more serious," Allison said.

Jesse laughed, then opened his car door. A few minutes later he and Allison stood at Maggie's front door.

"Jesse…Cecilia. How nice to see you both." Maggie greeted them in surprise. "Come in, please." She grabbed Allison's arm in a warm grasp and led her over to the sofa.

"We just thought we'd stop in and see how you are doing," Allison said, aware of Maggie sitting down next to her.

"Is there any news…? I mean, have you found out who…?" Maggie's voice trailed off.

"No, Maggie. No news, but I'm still working on it," Jesse said regretfully. "I promise we'll get him, no matter how long it takes."

Loud footsteps echoed down the stairs and Allison felt the air stir as another person entered the room.

"Sheriff…ma'am," a deep, gravelly voice greeted them.

"Landry." Jesse returned the greeting.

"You gonna catch the son of a bitch that hurt Maggie?"

"I'm doing everything I can to get him," Jesse replied.

"Why don't we take a little walk outside, give the ladies a chance to prattle alone?"

"Yes, we have some girl talk to exchange," Allison said.

"Heaven save us from girl talk," Burt replied. "Come on, Sheriff. We'll go out back. I've got a six-pack on ice in the cooler."

Allison waited a moment until the men had left the room, then she reached for Maggie's hands. "How are you really?"

"I'm doing okay," Maggie replied. "I have good moments and bad moments. Nights are the hardest. I sometimes have bad dreams."

"Amanda is worried about you."

"Amanda is a good friend." Allison could hear the smile in Maggie's voice.

"She thinks you're making a mistake getting back with Burt."

"I might be...." Maggie pulled her hands from Allison's and released a deep sigh. "Burt can be difficult. He drinks too much, he's loud and obnoxious, he can be mean-spirited...."

"Then why are you getting back with him?" Allison asked softly.

There was a long silence. "Have you ever been truly afraid and just felt like you needed somebody—anybody—to hang on to? Not necessarily forever, but just for now?" She reached once again for Allison's hands, then laughed a bit unsteadily. "Burt is no prize, but he's been good to me since...since the rape. I just need him to hang on to right now."

As Allison and Maggie talked about upcoming social activities in town and general things, Maggie's words played and replayed in Allison's head.

Have you ever been truly afraid and just felt like you needed somebody—anybody—to hang on to?

Did that explain Allison's overwhelming attraction to Jesse? An any-port-in-a-storm mentality? Was it an attraction based on the overwhelming uncertainty of her life?

What right did she have to question Maggie's choice of hanging on to Burt for all the wrong reasons when it was just possible she was doing the very same thing with Jesse?

Jesse hadn't liked Burt Landry the first time he talked to him, and this second little male bonding session hadn't improved his attitude toward the handsome, burly cowboy.

"So, I tell her…hell, little lady, if you want to ride a real bucking bronco, come on home with me tonight." Landry guffawed loudly, then drained his second beer and tossed the can aside. "Sure I can't tempt you?" he asked as he reached into the cooler for another brew.

"No, thanks. We need to be heading out. Besides, I'm on duty and I've got to get down to the station and check things out."

"Yeah, I guess this Casanova thing has you really jumping." Burt shook his head. "Damnedest thing, isn't it? What kind of pervert takes girls out to a tree and kisses them? Sounds damn dumb to me." He took a sip of his beer. "But I guess the reward might turn up something."

"Reward?" Jesse frowned in bewilderment. "What reward?"

"It was in the paper this morning. Millicent Creighton and that bunch of old ladies she calls her Ladies' Club have put up a thousand-dollar reward for information leading to the capture of Casanova."

Jesse stifled a curse. Terrific. Just terrific. "I'd better get to the station," he said. With a nod of goodbye to Landry, he reentered the house to get Allison.

"Every nut in the county will be calling in about their weird brother, or estranged ex-husband or the crazy kid next door," Jesse fumed a few minutes later as he drove Allison back to his house. "Damn Millicent and her stupid stunts. We'll be kept busy for the next month running down dead-end leads."

"I'm sure she thought she was just being help-ful," Allison said.

Jesse sighed. "I know that, Allison. But this re-ward thing only complicates the investigation." Jesse tightened his grip on the steering wheel and shot a glance sideways as he recognized his mistake in calling her by her real name.

He had to stop thinking of Cecilia as Allison. She should have never told him her real name the night before. It complicated things more than they al-ready were. Now he'd have to be careful and make sure he didn't call her Allison in public.

He pulled into his driveway. "I'll get the car un-loaded, then call Shelly to come over and stay with you. I'll probably spend most of the evening down at the station." She nodded, seeming distant and preoccupied. "Everything was okay with Maggie?" he asked. "Cecilia?"

"What?" She turned her beautiful, blank eyes in his direction. "Oh, yes. She's doing as well as can be expected. This thing with Burt... She knows what she's doing. She needs him right now." She opened her car door, as if that ended their discussion.

Back in the house, she disappeared into the bathroom for a shower while Jesse called the station and talked to Shelly before going back outside to unload the camping equipment. As he worked, his mind whirled a million miles a minute.

Making love to Allison last night had probably been a mistake. And for a few minutes that morning, he'd worried about what her reaction would be to their night of lovemaking. But when she'd told him not to worry, that for her it had been nothing but a pleasant release of energy, he'd wanted to shout a protest.

It had been so much more than simply a physical release. Making love with Allison had awakened something deep in Jesse's soul...a need he hadn't realized he possessed, dreams he hadn't realized might be within his grasp.

"Crazy," he muttered, wondering if sex made all men think foolish thoughts. Did the surge of testosterone zap brain cells?

By the time he finished unloading the camping gear, the dark clouds that had appeared that morning had usurped the last of the blue sky.

He went into the house, surprised to find Allison

had sandwiches waiting. "I thought you should eat before you went to the station," she said. "It's nothing fancy, just bologna and cheese with a little mustard."

"Thanks." He sat at the table, touched by her thoughtfulness. "Bologna and cheese is just fine."

She smelled of soap and shampoo and the faint odor of spring flowers. Her dark hair was still damp from her shower but glistened with rich highlights.

As always, she wore blue jeans and a blue T-shirt. "How come you always wear blue?" he asked.

She sat at the table next to him. "When I left the hospital, a police woman went shopping for me. She thought it would be easy for me to coordinate my clothing if everything was the same color." She smiled, an impish teasing lighting her eyes. "That way I don't look like your living room."

"My living room?"

"Yeah, you know...all purple plaid and green stripes or whatever you said when you described it to me."

Jesse laughed and she joined him. "If you think the living room is bad, you should see my bedroom."

"Don't tell me," she protested, then laughed. "Okay...go ahead and tell me."

"Wallpaper with huge pink and yellow roses, and it's peeling."

"Have you no shame?" she teased. "Why on earth haven't you done something about it?"

"I don't know. I really hate it, but I just haven't

gotten around to doing anything. Normally I don't spend much time here.''

''But this is your home, a place where you should surround yourself with colors and fabrics that comfort you.''

He laughed. ''Now you're talking like an interior decorator.''

''I *am* an interior decorator.''

With those simple words, Jesse was reminded that no matter what he'd felt last night when he'd held her in his arms and made love to her, he and Mustang were temporary for her.

And in that instant, Jesse knew what he wanted. Before she left Mustang, before she left his life for good, he wanted to see her wearing something green—something silky and in the same wonderful shade as her eyes.

At that moment Shelly arrived. Jesse wrapped the remainder of his sandwich in a paper towel and escaped, grateful that Shelly had shown up before he said or did anything stupid.

As he drove away from the house, he thought of what she'd said about his house, about it being his home and being filled with things that comforted him.

He'd never really thought of the house as a home. A home implied warmth and companionship. A home should contain a husband and wife, two people committed to building a life together, facing the future side by side.

He'd never really wanted to build a home. His house had always been enough for him—a place to eat, sleep and shower. Allison's presence in his house had subtly transformed things.

Hc liked knowing that when he pulled into the driveway the porch light was on for him. He liked knowing that when he walked through the door if he wanted to talk, she would listen.

He tightened his grip on the steering wheel as his mind filled with visions of Allison. He could still taste the sweetness of her kisses on his lips, feel the heated touch of her hands on his skin. She had been far more passionate, far more giving than he'd dreamed.

And what irritated him more than anything was the fact that even though he knew it was wrong, remembering those moments of intense intimacy evoked an overwhelming desire to repeat the experience.

Chapter 10

Allison stood in front of the dresser mirror in her bedroom, brushing her hair before getting into bed. Despite the fact she couldn't see her reflection, she supposed it was the lingering of a lifetime habit that she always stood in front of the mirror.

It had been a long, quiet evening. Shelly had been depressed because she couldn't get Sam to acknowledge her as anything but a partner. "Unrequited lust stinks," she'd announced before falling into a depressed pout.

Allison had been quiet, as well, working through her own feelings, trying to separate emotion from intellect and desire from need. Maggie's words haunted her, forcing her to examine all the emotions she felt for Jesse.

By the time Jesse had returned home for the night

thirty minutes ago, Allison's thoughts were no clearer and she decided to go to bed.

Her feelings about Jesse were confusing. She didn't know if she was falling in love with Jesse because he represented safety and security. If she could see and if her world were normal, would she feel the same way about him?

She paused, hairbrush in the air. She was falling in love with Jesse. The sound of rumbling thunder drifted into her open window, as if to underscore the drama of her sudden realization.

She sank onto the edge of the bed, her heart thudding rapidly.

Jesse. He made her laugh, he made her feel safe, and last night he'd made her body sing with sensations she'd never felt before. It frightened her just a little, because she didn't know if she could trust the feelings.

There were too many other variables between them for her to be certain of her own emotions. She was suffering hysterical blindness, was miles away from her own home. She'd come to Mustang, Montana, seeking shelter and safety.

Her growing feelings for Jesse felt real, but could she trust her own emotions when there was so much turbulence in her head, so much fear and grief and uncertainty in her heart? She didn't know the answer.

She stood and once again approached the dresser, but hesitated as a sound drifted in through the open window. She froze. Her heart suddenly pounded in a much different way than it had seconds before.

The noise she'd heard had sounded like footsteps breaking foliage. Along with the noise came the distinct feeling that she wasn't alone, that somebody was nearby.

"Is somebody there?" she asked. There was another audible snap of brush, a faint grunt, and this noise broke her initial paralysis.

She threw open her bedroom door, crying out in pain as something hit her cheek and forehead. "Jesse," she yelled at the same time she realized something hadn't hit her but rather she'd walked into the edge of the door in her haste.

Jesse's bedroom door flew open. "Allison, what's wrong?"

"I think somebody is outside my bedroom window."

He asked no further questions. He took her by the shoulders and moved her down the hallway near the bathroom door.

"Stay here," he commanded. "I'll go check it out." His words were punctuated by another clap of thunder, this one louder, closer.

Allison crossed her arms over her chest and hugged her shoulders, fear rising, consuming her. Had they found her? The men—the officers who had murdered Alicia, murdered John... Had they found her safe haven...? Had they come here to kill her, too?

Where was Jesse? What was taking him so long? The seconds transformed to minutes in agonizing tempo. What was taking so long? What was happening? Where was Jesse? Please, please don't let anything happen to Jesse, her mind screamed.

Fear transformed to terror as flashes of memory tormented her. Alicia...John...the sound of gunshots. I can't let them see me, Allison thought. The closet...the closet is safe...they can't find me in the dark. The dark is a good place to hide.

"Allison, it's okay, honey."

Jesse's voice sliced through the terror, banishing it like a surgeon's knife cutting away a tumor. Allison realized that in her fear she had once again sought the safety of her closet. She was huddled on the floor, pressed into the corner. Without conscious knowledge, her body had carried her to the place that had kept her safe once before.

Jesse's hand touched one of hers, and she held on tightly as she left the safe confines of the small, dark space.

The moment she could straighten, she pressed against him. She wrapped her arms around him and held tight, allowing the last vestiges of fear to leave her body.

She stood for a long moment in his embrace, the scent of him comfortable and familiar, the warmth of his skin a reassuring sign of life and safety.

Thunder once again rumbled overhead, this time not sounding like gunshots, but simply the approach of a storm. "You didn't find anybody?" she asked, her face pressed against his bare chest.

She fought the need to press her lips against him, fought the desire to taste his skin and lose herself and forget her fear in a dizzying whirl of desire.

"No, I didn't see anyone. I checked the yard, the neighbors' yards and down the block."

She released him and stepped back, embarrassment replacing fear. "I guess I just imagined it. Maybe the thunder made me think I was hearing things."

He took her hand and guided her to the bed where she sat. "You didn't imagine anything," he said, his voice tight with tension. "Apparently somebody was outside your window. The rosebush beneath the window was half-trampled."

"That's what I heard," she exclaimed. "I heard crackling, like brush breaking."

She rubbed her arms, suddenly cold as she thought of somebody standing at the window, watching her as she brushed her hair. Had somebody been there when she'd changed into her nightgown? Had they watched her as she'd undressed?

Dear God, had there been a gun pointed in her direction? Had somebody been waiting for the perfect shot? Or had they intended to wait until she was sleeping, then sneak in the window and silently cut her throat?

"Do you think they've found me? The Renegade Eight from Chicago?" Her voice was whisper soft.

Jesse didn't reply immediately. She sensed him moving in front of her, pacing like a caged wild animal. "I don't know," he finally said. "I only know that somebody was there."

"Maybe we should call Kent Keller or Bob Sandford and see what's happening. Maybe they could tell us if somebody knows where I am…if—''

''I can't do that,'' Jesse interrupted her. ''They told me they'd contact me.''

''But this changes things,'' she replied, her voice slightly shrill. ''We have a right to know what's going on. We need to know if anyone has gotten information about me. We need to know if they know where I am.''

Jesse sat next to her and once again took her hand in his. ''Allison, I can't call those men because if I do there will be a record of the call. If nobody knows where you are, but people are looking for you, calling is too dangerous. If Bob or Kent's calls are secretly being monitored, a call from me might put you in extreme danger.''

Allison once again rubbed her arms as a chill swept through her. ''I hadn't thought of that,'' she admitted.

''Here's something else to consider,'' Jesse said. ''It's possible whoever was looking in your window has nothing to do with what happened in Chicago.''

Allison sat up in surprise, recognizing he could be right. ''Casanova!'' she exclaimed.

''Exactly.'' He released a deep sigh. ''Come on, let's go to the kitchen and get something to eat. I have a feeling it's going to take us both a little while to wind down enough to sleep.'' Before they left the room, Jesse shut and locked her window, then pulled the curtains tightly closed.

Moments later they sat at the table, a bag of chips and a couple of sodas in front of them. Allison couldn't eat, although she sipped her soda, trying to remove the taste of horror that lingered in her mouth. The idea that somebody had stood at the window and peeked in at her without her knowledge made her feel violated.

"I hate the idea of somebody watching me and me being unable to see them," she said, breaking the heavy silence that had fallen between them.

"Thank God you heard them and had the presence of mind to call for me." Jesse's voice was deeper than usual and Allison knew he must be wondering what would have happened had she fallen asleep with the window open. She'd been wondering the same thing.

Would somebody have crept through the window, their actions hidden in the darkness of her blindness and any noise concealed by the thunder and the storm? Who had been there?

Jesse's hand enfolded hers. "Don't think about it," he said, as if he were able to read her mind.

"I can't help but think about it," she replied. Nor could she ignore the pleasure of his touch. His hand warmed her heart, swept away the fear and replaced it with the certainty of his protection.

Jesse released her hand and instead touched the side of her face. She winced. "What did you do?" he asked. "You have a scrape here."

"When I yanked open my door to call for you, I walked into it. It's fine, just a little tender."

She frowned thoughtfully. "Is it possible Casanova watched his other victims before he actually committed his crimes?"

"I don't know. None of the other women mentioned anything unusual happening before the night Casanova visited them. And believe me, I asked."

"I think if the person outside the window was one of the Renegade Eight, I wouldn't be sitting here eating chips with you," Allison said thoughtfully. "I think one of those dirty cops would have shot me and disappeared into the night."

"I think you're probably right," Jesse agreed. He released her hand and she fought the impulse to reach for him once again.

"So that means it was possible that Casanova was watching me…perhaps waiting for me to go to sleep with an open, unlocked window."

"Yeah, it's possible." Jesse's voice was filled with suppressed fury. "If it was Casanova, then the son of a bitch is getting bolder. I'm the sheriff, for God's sake, and for all intents and purposes you're my fiancée."

He was quiet for a moment, then continued. "Maybe we're jumping to conclusions. It's possible Jed Burnside was peeking into the window."

"Jed Burnside?" Allison frowned. "Who's that?"

"Jed is Mustang's resident Peeping Tom. He's sixty-nine years old and maintains that open curtains are an invitation to peep. I'll talk to him tomorrow."

"But if it wasn't this Jed…and it was Casanova, maybe we can catch him," Allison said. She leaned forward. "If he's focused in on me, then maybe we should let him take me."

"You mean use you as bait? Absolutely not." His chair scooted noisily against the floor at the same time thunder clapped overhead and rain began to pelt the windows.

"Jesse, it might be the way to finally catch him." She leaned forward eagerly. Suddenly it felt like the one thing she could do to repay him for all he had done for her. "We could do it, Jesse. We could set it up, entice him."

"I said no, and I mean no." He scooted back his chair and stood, his voice nearly as loud as the last boom of thunder. "There are too many factors we can't control. I can't take the risk. I won't let you take the risk." His voice had softened. "I couldn't live with myself if something went wrong, if you were harmed."

Allison's heart swelled with his words. He cared about her. She could hear it in his voice, felt it in the tension that radiated from him.

"Allison, you've been placed in my care for protection, and I take that responsibility very seriously. I would be remiss in my duty to intentionally place you in harm's way. It won't be done."

These words punctured the swell of her heart. Of course he cared about her—like a baby-sitter cared for little charges, like a mechanic cared for a car. A job.

They had momentarily blurred the lines between duty and desire the night before, but Allison would do well to remember her place in Jesse's life—she was a temporary responsibility and nothing more.

* * *

Jesse grabbed a chip from the bag, his mind whirling in a million different directions as he ate it. Somebody had been outside Allison's window and his gut told him it had been Casanova.

Before he'd found Allison hiding in the closet, he'd called the station and alerted the deputies on duty. At this moment they should be patrolling the neighborhood, looking for anyone suspicious. But Jesse didn't expect them to find anyone.

He grabbed another chip, trying to keep his attention off the fact that Allison was clad in her silky blue nightgown and robe. The robe was unbelted and hung loose down her sides, displaying the low-cut nightgown that exposed her beautiful long neck and the tops of her creamy breasts.

It had been less than twenty-four hours since they'd made love and yet Jesse felt like a man starving for her. He wanted to wrap himself around her, hear her throaty sighs as he possessed her, watch her eyes as they lit with passion...passion for him.

He frowned and took a sip of his soda. It filled him with rage to think that Casanova might attempt to hurt Allison.

He'd been angered to see the three victims, their pain and trauma. He'd been angered to see the women of his town filled with fear. But this possible threat to Allison pulled his anger into a new dimension.

A knock resounded on the door. Jesse and Allison both jumped up from their chairs. "That's probably one of my men," Jesse said. "I have them patrolling the area."

Allison followed close behind him to the door. Before answering it, Jesse turned to her. Gently he pulled the robe more closely around her and belted it. Someplace in the back of his mind, he was aware that he didn't want anyone to see her as he just had, with so much skin exposed and looking so incredibly lovely.

"Thanks," she murmured, her cheeks stained a delicate pink.

He peered through the peephole, then opened the door to see Vic, dripping rainwater from the brim of his hat. "Come in." He grabbed the burly man's arm and pulled him into the house and out of the storm.

"It's turning into a real toad-strangler," Vic said as he brushed droplets from his shoulders. "Hi, Cecilia."

"Hi, Vic." She returned the greeting with a warm smile.

"See anything?" Jesse asked, cutting to the chase.

Vic shook his head. "Nothing. We cruised all over the area, looked in yards, inside sheds... wherever somebody might hide."

Jesse sighed. "That's what I figured. Thanks for coming out on a night like this."

Vic shrugged his broad shoulders. "Hey, it's my job."

He looked at Allison. "You doing okay, Cecilia?"

"I'm fine, Vic. It was just a little disconcerting to know somebody might have been watching me."

She smiled. "From now on my curtains will stay drawn and my window shut and locked."

"That would probably be wise," Vic agreed. He took a step back toward the door. "I'll get out of here. Just wanted to check in and let you know we've come up empty-handed."

"Thanks again, Vic. I'll see you tomorrow." Jesse closed and locked the door after the deputy, then turned to Allison. "It's getting late. Don't you think you should go to bed?"

She shook her head. "I'm still too wound up for sleep. But you go on if you want to. I'll just sit here for a little while." She sank onto the sofa.

"I'll sit with you for a while longer," he replied, and sat in the chair opposite her. For a long moment they sat in silence, the only sound in the room the gentle patter of rain against the windows.

"Jesse? Would you tell me about Paul?"

Her question made him jerk upright with surprise. "Paul? How do you know anything about Paul?"

"Shelly mentioned something about him."

Irritation swept through Jesse. Why on earth would Shelly mention Paul to Allison? And yet, even as the question fluttered through his mind, the answer was obvious.

"What do you want to know?" he asked grudgingly.

"Tell me about him...and about you." She leaned forward, as if eager to hear what he had to say.

He didn't want to do this. He was tired, and

thinking about Paul always brought up a strange melancholy, a pain deep inside his heart he never addressed.

"There's not much to tell. We were friends, we had an accident, he moved away and we lost touch." It was a recitation of facts void of emotion.

"You were close…friends for a long time before the accident?" she asked, apparently unaware that she was digging into unhealed wounds.

Jesse leaned back into the chair, memories suddenly unfolding in his head. "Paul and I became best friends in second grade and we remained best friends throughout high school. We did almost everything together, were rarely apart. I loved Paul like a brother." A lump of pressure tightened Jesse's chest.

"What happened the night of the accident?"

Again memories assailed Jesse. The party…the music…the laughter, then the black night, the icy roads and the crunch of metal and shattering of glass.

"We'd been to a party." He used his fingers to rub the center of his forehead where a headache had begun to knock. "About halfway through the party, Paul started bugging me to go home. The weather was turning nasty and it had begun to sleet."

"But you didn't want to go home," she said softly.

He looked at her in surprise, wondering how a blind woman could see so much. "That's right," he agreed. "I was feeling my oats that night. Carolina McKenzie, a cute junior, was flirting with me and I didn't want to leave early. The storm didn't bother me. I was feeling indestructible...completely invincible.''

''As do most teenagers.''

''I suppose.'' Again Jesse rubbed his forehead, his headache growing more intense. He didn't want to go back to that night, and yet felt as if he were powerless to stop the momentum of his memory, and perhaps a need to finally talk about what had happened.

''We left the party and at first the roads weren't too terribly bad. Slick...but negotiable.'' He paused, seeking some sort of distance from the horror, but the horror refused to release him. The memories were as vivid as if the accident had happened the night before.

He swallowed hard, then continued. ''We'd only gone a few miles when the sleet and ice came down in earnest. The minute we crested the hill, I knew I was no longer in control.''

He got up and began to pace, unable to sit immobile any longer. ''I practically stood on the brakes, but it did no good. We went faster and faster down the hill. I couldn't steer...I couldn't slow down. It was like being on a roller coaster. I wasn't in control.''

Again the pressure filled his chest, pressing so hard he had difficulty drawing breath. ''We saw the tree long before we hit it. We both knew we were going to hit it because we were going so fast...so damned fast.''

The words tumbled from him now, like a speeding locomotive unable to stop its frantic forward motion. "We hit the tree and I think I must have blacked out for a moment. When I came to, the front window was gone and so was Paul." He sank down next to Allison, afraid his legs would no longer hold him as he remembered.

She grabbed his hands and held them tight, as if recognizing the tremendous emotion that had loosened inside him. "I found him beneath the tree, covered with branches that had broken when his body had careened into it. I thought he was dead. Oh, God...his face...his face was covered with blood. And his eyes...they looked as if they weren't there."

Allison released his hands and instead drew him into an embrace. He closed his eyes, vaguely wondering how it was possible that her arms around him could ease somewhat his pain. "It was an accident, Jesse. A terrible accident, but you weren't responsible."

He pulled away from her, amazed that she could say such a thing, think such a thing. "But I was responsible," he said, his pain evident in the choked quality of his voice. "I should have listened to Paul when he said we should leave the party. Had we left earlier, the accident would have never happened."

"You can't know that," she admonished. "If I'd taken John and Alicia out to dinner that night, they wouldn't have been murdered. If I'd driven my car instead of taken a taxi, perhaps the murderers wouldn't have entered their house. If...if... You can't go there, Jesse. You're the one who told me that." She sat back from him and appeared to be looking right at him, right into his very soul. "Jesse, you have no reason to feel guilty. It was a terrible accident, but it wasn't your fault."

He said nothing. On an intellectual level, he knew she was right. On an emotional level, there were times his guilt threatened to consume him. He released a shuddering sigh. "This is the first time I've ever really talked about the accident other than with the officers who finally responded to the scene."

"And what happened between you and Paul afterward?" Once again he found his hands in hers, as if she intended to give him strength.

"Nothing. I went to the hospital the next day and Paul's parents met me in the waiting room. They told me they thought it best if I not see Paul."

"That must have been very hurtful."

He nodded, but a renewed sense of guilt rose up inside him, guilt because coupled with the hurt had been intense relief. "I never saw Paul again after the accident. His family remained in Mustang only for a brief time, then they moved to a neighboring town."

Jesse pulled his hands from hers and stood, more tired than he could ever remember being. "I think I'm going to call it a night. We've both had enough excitement and emotion for one evening."

"Go ahead," she said, not moving from the sofa. "You can turn off the lights. I'll go to bed when I'm ready."

Jesse looked at her for a long moment. Somehow he felt as if she'd seen into his heart, had known he needed to talk about Paul. Some of the pressure, the heaviness of his heart that he'd carried for years, had eased.

"Good night, Allison," he said softly.

What he wanted to do was take her by the arm, lead her into his bedroom and make love to her. He wanted to sleep with her wrapped around him, awaken with her body warming his. He knew the foolishness of such wants, and so instead he went to his room alone.

He took off his clothes, turned out the light and got into his bed, his thoughts sliding back to Paul. When his relationship with Paul had ended, something inside Jesse had died—the part of him that was soft and vulnerable, the part of him that was capable of love.

He suddenly realized he'd spent his adult years being afraid of growing too close to anyone, afraid of caring, then losing somebody important to him. He suddenly realized how empty his life had been, and he'd never felt utterly lonely until this very moment.

Closing his eyes, he drew a deep breath, trying to shove aside all thoughts so that the blessed peace of sleep could claim him.

"Jesse?"

He opened his eyes to see Allison's shadowy form standing in his doorway. "Yeah?"

"I'm afraid to sleep in that room. Could I sleep with you? I—I need you."

Jesse's heart filled his chest. Without saying a word, he got up, took her hand and led her to his bed because God help him, he needed her, too.

Chapter 11

Allison refused to think about the many emotions that had brought her once again to Jesse's bed. She only knew it was where she wanted to be. She needed him and she knew he needed her, too.

The moment she slid beneath the sheets, he met her with a hungry kiss that made any further thought impossible. She responded with a hunger of her own.

The fear she'd felt when she'd realized somebody was outside the window melted away beneath the heat of his mouth. She hoped that in some way her kiss, her warmth, her love would ease the anguish he'd felt in relating the accident with Paul.

When the kiss finally ended, they were both breathless, passions instantly heightened to overwhelming proportions. Allison took off her nightgown, wanting to be as close—as intimate—as possible with him.

When he reached for her again, he was naked, as well, his desire evident. His body felt fevered as he drew her back against him. It was a fever she wanted to lose herself in.

His mouth possessed hers again as his hands found her breasts. Allison moaned, his touch an exquisite torment. He teased her nipples, his fingers dancing lightly across the taut peaks.

As they kissed, she ran her fingers over his forehead, across his brow, down his angular face, seeing him with her fingertips, memorizing him in her mind. Although she couldn't really know him visually, she knew him in her heart.

Whereas before they had made love slowly, with tentative, explorative caresses, this time they were both ready without any prolonged foreplay.

As Jesse moved into her, she welcomed him, her hands clutching his back. She'd only made love to him once before, but she felt a sense of sweet familiarity, a sense of homecoming as he moved with her in the rhythm of passion.

His heartbeat raced against hers, his breath warmed her neck as he took her higher…closer to the edge. All thought was impossible as she gave herself to him, allowing him to completely possess her.

She cried out as wave after wave of pleasure swept through her, and he stiffened against her and hoarsely cried her name as he, too, tumbled over the edge.

Later, as she lay in his arms, she realized she'd been wrong earlier in the evening. When she'd stood in the bedroom and worried about falling in love with Jesse, it had already been too late. She'd fallen hard.

Snuggling against his body, she realized the exact moment she'd crossed the line from falling in love to being in love. It had been when he'd gently tied her robe before opening the door to admit Vic.

In that single, simple act of thoughtfulness, he'd captured the essence of her soul, stolen the core of her heart.

She didn't know what to do about it. He had spoken no words of love, had not indicated in any way that she was anything more than a pleasant physical diversion and a required job.

Knowing there was no way to sort out her feelings now, while in his warm embrace and with the scent of him lingering on her skin, she closed her eyes and allowed herself to drift to sleep.

When she awakened again, he was gone. She had no idea what time it was, but knew it must be morning because she felt fully rested. She reached out and touched Jesse's pillow. The pillowcase was cold, retaining no residual body warmth. Jesse must have left some time ago.

She remained beneath the sheets that smelled of him, wondering how it was possible to be so filled with the joy of love and the ache of anticipated loss at the same time.

She grabbed his pillow and hugged it against her chest, as if it were him she held on to so tightly.

If she could see, would she still love Jesse? Yes. Her love for him had no basis in what he looked like, in the clothes he wore or how he carried himself.

But at least for the moment she couldn't see. And her blindness complicated everything.

She released her hold on his pillow and got out of bed. She felt around on the floor for the gown she'd discarded the night before. After several moments of searching, she found it on the edge of the bed. Jesse must have placed it there, where it would be easy for her to find, before he left. Again her heart expanded as she embraced the notion of his thoughtfulness.

She pulled it on, then went across the hall to her own bedroom. The scent of fresh brewed coffee wafted down the hallway and she assumed Shelly was probably sitting in the kitchen, waiting for Allison to join her for morning gossip and brew.

After a quick shower, Allison dressed in a pair of jeans and a T-shirt, then left her room and went into the kitchen. The moment she stepped foot into the room, she knew it wasn't Shelly sitting at the table.

"Vic?" she said hesitantly.

"Wow, how did you do that?" His deep voice held utter amazement.

She smiled and sat at the table across from where she knew he must be sitting. "Jesse's cologne is distinctive and Shelly wears a perfume with a vanilla base. You smell clean, like soap...which reminds me, I haven't had a chance to thank you for the lovely soap fish sculpture."

"Ah, it was nothing, just something I do in my spare time."

"You must be getting less spare time since I've been here." She got up and made her way to the counter for a cup of coffee. "I mean, you're pulling double duty or something to be here this morning after working so late last night."

"I don't mind," he said. "My job is pretty much my life." He hesitated a moment, then continued. "Jesse confided in me...you know, about what you're really doing here."

Allison nodded, not surprised that Jesse would divulge the truth to his trusted deputy. She poured herself a cup of coffee, then returned to the table. "So you know the engagement is all pretend, made up as a cover story."

"Yeah, Jesse explained all that." Vic's chair creaked as he shifted positions. "You're really brave. I have a lot of admiration for what you're doing."

"What I'm doing?"

"You know...testifying against a bunch of cops. Most people would walk away from the whole thing and refuse to cooperate in the investigation. They'd be too afraid to come forward."

Allison ran the tip of her finger around the rim of her cup. "I never considered not cooperating. Unfortunately my vision is being most uncooperative."

"What happens if your sight doesn't return before the trial?"

"It will." Allison's voice held a flat finality. She refused to consider any other option. Her sight would return. Any minute...any day, she would suddenly see again. She had to believe that.

She sipped her coffee, then smiled once again in Vic's direction. "Have you known Jesse for a long time?"

"Sure, Jesse and I went to school together, although we really didn't run in the same crowd. Jesse was a jock...you know, into football and basketball. I never did well at sports."

"Did you know Paul?" she asked.

"You mean Paul Burke?" She nodded and Vic continued. "Sure, everyone knew Paul. He was the golden boy, our star quarterback. He and Jesse were thick as thieves until the car accident."

"When Paul was blinded."

"That's right. You know, I never thought about it before now, but maybe you being here is sort of like karma," Vic said.

"Karma?"

"Yeah. Jesse was pretty torn up about Paul for a long time after the accident and he never really got a chance to resolve the whole thing. Maybe fate sent you here so Jesse could take care of you, and somehow that evens things up between him and Paul." Vic laughed, his deep voice tinged with a hint of embarrassment. "Guess that sounds sort of stupid, doesn't it?"

"No, it doesn't," Allison protested. She had

heard Jesse's pain and his guilt as he'd talked about Paul. She had a feeling Vic was right in that Jesse had a lot of unresolved feelings where Paul was concerned.

However, she didn't want to be the catalyst of his healing. She wanted him to care about her despite her blindness, not because of it.

She and Vic finished a pot of coffee and small-talked. Vic entertained her with stories about past investigations and criminals. When the conversation lagged, Allison excused herself and went into her bedroom.

Once there, she paced back and forth on the carpeting at the foot of the bed, wondering when Kent Keller would call, when her presence would be required in Chicago, when her time here in Mustang would end.

Jesse came home just after noon and sent Vic home. "There's a town meeting tonight," Jesse said to Allison, who was sitting on the sofa listening to a soap opera when he'd come home. "Most of the town usually turns out for these things and I have to be there. I'd like it if you go with me."

"Sure," she replied flippantly. "After all, we need to keep up appearances...the dutiful wife-to-be and all that." There was an edge of sarcasm in her voice that she hadn't intended. The weight of her love for him battled with the knowledge that they had no future together.

Jesse was silent for a long moment. "You don't have to go with me if you don't want to."

Shame washed over Allison. "Of course I'll go."

She waved her hands dismissively. "Don't mind me. I just had a moment of crankiness."

"I forgive you...as long as it's an isolated moment in time." His voice was filled with good-natured humor. "I brought you a present," he said.

"A present?"

He placed a large dress box on her lap. "Yeah, consider it an early or late birthday present."

"Early. My birthday is next month." She removed the top of the box and pulled aside a layer of tissue paper. Her fingers encountered material...the slick cool of silk.

"It's a dress," he said before she could ask. "I thought maybe you'd wear it to the town meeting tonight."

"Oh, Jesse, it feels beautiful." She smiled at him. "And I'll bet it isn't blue."

"You bet right. It's green, and I hope it's the right size."

"I'm sure it's fine," she assured him, touched that he'd gone to the trouble to get her something. She frowned as a new worry niggled in the back of her brain. "Jesse, did you buy this for me because my clothes look so bad?"

"No!" He sat next to her. "Not at all. You always look nice. I just thought...I wanted..." He stumbled over himself and Allison heard embarrassment in his voice. "I wanted you to have a green dress, something to match your eyes," he finally confessed.

He stood. "It's not a big deal, I just wanted you

to have it. I've got some calls to make. I'll talk to you later.''

Allison knew by the direction of his footsteps that he'd gone into the kitchen. Again Allison's fingers danced over the material, her heart as warm as the silk was cool.

He'd bought her a dress. A green dress to match her eyes.

Was that the action of a man who thought of her only as a job? As his duty? Or was that the action of a man who harbored a well of grief and guilt about a past trauma and was now using her to heal that pain?

This thought caused the warmth in her heart to cool to the temperature of the fabric.

Jesse sat up straighter in the wooden chair, trying to keep his attention focused on Elena Richards, who was discussing the possibility of a bronze statue for the city park.

The town meeting had been going on for about an hour, but Jesse had found concentration difficult from the moment Allison had walked out of her bedroom wearing the silk green dress.

She'd been more beautiful than he'd imagined. The dress fit her as if tailored just for her, emphasizing her slender waist and the full curve of her breasts. The full skirt swirled around her knees, exposing slender, shapely calves.

But it was the color that lit her up. The deep green perfectly matched her eyes and complemented the rich gleam of her hair. And in that first moment of seeing her, Jesse had realized his feelings for her went far beyond duty and deeper than desire.

He stirred, wishing she weren't sitting next to him, wishing he couldn't smell her perfume, feel her body heat where their thighs touched.

He was in love with her, and he didn't like the way she made him feel. He was anxious... joyous...nervous...excited, and beneath those myriad emotions was the certainty that eventually she would disappear from his life, leaving him only the memories of her wearing the damnable green dress and the feel of her in his arms.

Casting her a surreptitious sideways look, his heart expanded with emotion. He loved her, but he didn't want to just be an option for her. She couldn't see, had no life to return to, and so might opt to remain in Mustang with him because she didn't know what else to do. No, that's not how he wanted it.

Her blindness bothered him only in that it bothered her. She refused to accept it, refused to acknowledge that it might be permanent and therefore refused to contemplate what the future might hold for her.

Frustration added itself into the mix of his emotions. Whether she stayed or left Mustang, he wanted—needed—to know she could adjust, make a life for herself even if she remained blind.

As Millicent Creighton stepped up to the podium, he directed his attention to her. He listened absently as she spoke about the upcoming fall festival and the plans for the event, including a carnival in the high school gymnasium for the children to enjoy.

Finally the meeting came to an end and Jesse and Allison joined the others near the refreshment table for a few minutes of social chatter.

"Would you like some punch?" he asked Allison.

"That would be nice," she agreed.

"There are also cookies."

"No, just punch is fine," she replied.

"I'll be right back." He touched her arm to assure her, then headed for the punch bowl. By the time he got two glasses of punch, Millicent, along with Marissa Crockett, had joined Allison.

"I couldn't believe it when Marissa told me you hadn't contacted her about flowers for your wedding ceremony," Millicent was saying as Jesse returned. "My dear, you just can't put these things off until the last minute and expect everything to be perfect. The magical day is approaching and you really must start making plans."

"Perhaps they've decided to go to another florist," Marissa said, obviously embarrassed by Millicent's usual steamroller tactics.

"No, that's not it at all," Allison assured them.

"It's my fault," Jesse interjected. He handed Allison her glass of punch then smiled at Marissa. "Cecilia has been after me to make time to go with her into your shop and pick out flowers, but work has been keeping me so busy."

Millicent held up her hands, the action causing the stuffed canary atop her straw hat to tilt precariously to the side. "Please, let's not mention that dreadful man and his horrible crimes."

Jesse nodded. The last thing he wanted to discuss was Casanova. "Anyway, we'll try to get in to talk with you in the next week or two," he said to Marissa.

Marissa nodded, then excused herself as Millicent turned back to Allison. "My dear, we are in desperate need for volunteers to help at the carnival. I know as the sheriff's new bride, you'll want to be one of our volunteers."

"Certainly," Allison agreed, although Jesse knew as well as she did that she probably wouldn't be in Mustang when the fall festival and the carnival took place.

"Wonderful," Millicent exclaimed, and pulled a small notebook from her purse. "Now, let me see where we need people. We need ticket sellers at the door." She frowned. "But that won't work, will it?" She scanned the notebook again. "And I don't think it would do to put you in charge of the shooting gallery."

"Probably not," Allison agreed, her cheeks growing more pink by the moment.

"Well, I'm sure we can come up with something," Millicent said as she closed her notebook. "I'll be in touch."

"Are you okay?" Jesse asked the moment Millicent had left them.

"Fine. I'm just a little tired."

"Come on, let's get out of here." He took her by the elbow and led her toward the door of the community building. Before they could make their exit, Vic appeared.

"Wow, don't you look nice," he said to Allison.

She smiled, her face lighting up with the gesture. Heat exploded in the pit of Jesse's stomach. The heat of desire. "Thanks, Vic," she replied. "And I'm sure you're looking just fine yourself, too."

Jesse was surprised to see the big deputy blush with pleasure at her words. "Ah, I just look normal," Vic exclaimed.

It would appear his deputy had developed a small crush on his fiancée, Jesse thought with a touch of amusement. The amusement fled as quickly as it had come.

She was not his fiancée, and why wouldn't Vic have a crush on her? Allison was not only beautiful, but genuinely nice, as well. Any man would be proud to have her in his life.

He would be proud to have her in his life. He frowned and took her by the arm. "We were just on our way out," he said to Vic.

"Oh, sure. Okay, I'll see you tomorrow." Vic nodded and headed toward the refreshment table.

They rode home in silence. Jesse had no idea what thoughts were playing through her head, but his was filled with irritation.

He was irritated with her, for being bright and beautiful and the kind of woman he could love. And he was irritated with himself, for allowing himself to fall in love with a woman who should have remained a job and nothing more.

She was a woman in transition—not a great bet

for forever. When Keller called, she'd be gone, back to a life in Chicago. He wasn't clear what that life would be if her blindness didn't abate, but she'd never indicated that she would consider a life here in Mustang.

He gripped the steering wheel more tightly. Besides, he'd promised himself a long time ago he would never allow his heart to be vulnerable to another person.

Better he keep his feelings for her to himself, better that he never hold her in his arms again, never kiss her sweet lips. It was time for him to distance himself and prepare for the time when she would walk out of his life and never look back.

When they walked into the house, the phone was ringing. Jesse raced for the phone while Allison sat on the sofa.

"Sheriff Wilder?" A familiar deep voice filled the line.

"Yes." Jesse listened intently to what Kent Keller had to say to him, then the two men said their goodbyes and hung up.

Jesse turned to Allison. "That was Kent Keller."

She leaned forward, tension instantly apparent in her posture. "And?"

"And it's all over. They've arrested not only the officers responsible for your sister's and brother-in-law's deaths, but also the rest of the Renegade Eight."

Her body sagged back against the sofa cushions. "Thank God," she whispered. "Now John and Alicia can rest in peace."

"There's more good news," he continued. "They're not going to need you to testify."

She frowned. "Why not?"

"Number one, for the obvious reason. Your sight hasn't returned, so you can't make a visual identification. A jury would certainly have problems believing your cyewitness testimony. Number two, they don't need you. One of the shooters is singing like a bird. For the offer of immunity, he's turning on his partners in crime."

"So it's finally over," she said.

Jesse was happy for her, but his happiness was tempered with the knowledge that there was nothing more to keep her in Mustang. "Kent will be here first thing in the morning on the day after tomorrow to take you home."

"Home." She echoed the word without enthusiasm and he wondered what was going on in her mind. Would she miss Mustang just a little? Miss him?

What difference does it make if she did miss him? A little voice whispered in the back of his mind. She needed to go home and get her life back on track.

In two days' time she'd be gone from his life. How ironic, that she'd been the one to pump life into his heart just in time to break it into little pieces.

Chapter 12

Home.

The following morning as Shelly chattered about her breakthrough with Sam, Allison thought about the fact that in twenty-four hours she was going home.

Home to a silent, lonely apartment. Home to a business she could no longer run. Home to a place that had never really felt like home.

When had this house in Mustang become her home? When had she begun to feel as if she belonged here...with Jesse? It didn't matter. She wasn't going to stay. She would return to Chicago with Kent Keller and try to pick up the pieces of the life she'd left behind.

Jesse deserved a woman who could be a productive volunteer at the yearly carnival. Her face burned as she thought of Millicent Creighton, desperately trying to figure out how Allison might be useful, helping out at the carnival. Allison had never felt so ineffectual, so useless in her life.

Jesse deserved a woman who could be a helpmate to him, not a liability. He deserved a woman who could add to his life, not further burden it.

She'd once again been bitterly disappointed when she'd opened her eyes that morning to the same veil of darkness. She'd thought with the murders solved and the bad guys in jail, her sight would miraculously return. But it hadn't happened.

"Anyway, so I told him he needed a real woman in his life, not another one of the bimbos he's been dating," Shelly said. "So tonight Sam is taking me out to dinner and to a movie." Shelly's voice was filled with her happiness.

Allison focused on Shelly's conversation. "Shelly, I'm so pleased for you. I know how much you like Sam," Allison replied.

"Yeah, the big lug has definitely captured my heart. Now all I have to do is by the end of tonight convince Sam I'm the only one for him."

Allison wanted to warn her to go slow, not to sleep with Sam until she had a ring on her finger and a commitment from him.

Sharing the kind of intimacy that sex involved made saying goodbye so much more difficult. Allison's heart ached with the knowledge that in twenty-four hours she would be saying goodbye to Jesse forever.

"How about some lunch?" Shelly asked. "I

could whip us up a big salad, or maybe heat up some soup."

"None for me. I'm not hungry," Allison said. Besides, before he'd left for work that morning, Jesse had said he'd be home for lunch. She'd much prefer to eat lunch with him, knowing it might be the last meal they shared. "But feel free to help yourself," she added.

"Nah, I'm not really hungry, either," Shelly replied. "I'm too excited about tonight to eat."

Allison realized she was going to miss Shelly. Shelly had not only been a guardian, but had become a friend, as well.

Allison had hated the fact that she hadn't been able to really confide in Shelly because of the threat to her life. Now she realized that threat had been removed and there was nothing keeping her from telling Shelly everything.

"Shelly, my name isn't Cecilia. My name is Allison Welch," she said.

"What are you talking about?" Shelly asked in surprise.

For the next few minutes, Allison told Shelly about the crime that occurred and the events that had ultimately brought her to Mustang and Jesse Wilder.

Shelly interrupted her from time to time to ask questions, obviously surprised by what Allison was telling her.

"I have to confess, you've depressed me," Shelly said when Allison had finished.

"Depressed you?"

"Yeah. I mean, you're leaving in the morning to go back to Chicago, and Chicago is a long way from here. That means we'll probably never see each other again." Shelly took Allison's hand in hers. "I feel like I'm losing a new friend."

Allison squeezed Shelly's hand, touched by her admission. "I'm going to miss you, too."

"So the engagement and the pending wedding between you and Jesse was all a ruse," Shelly said, releasing her hand. "Wow, you guys should be awarded a trophy for your acting skills. I mean, I've seen you two together, and I could have sworn what I saw in Jesse's eyes when he looks at you is love."

Her words caused unexpected tears to spring to Allison's eyes. "I'm sorry." Allison forced a self-conscious laugh and quickly swiped at her eyes.

"Oh, my gosh. It wasn't pretend for you, was it? You're in love with Jesse." It was not a question, but rather a statement of fact.

Again, tears filled Allison's eyes. "Yes, I am," she whispered, as if speaking the words aloud might shatter the last of her control.

"Have you told him?" Shelly asked.

Allison shook her head. "No, and I don't intend to."

"Why not? Don't you think he deserves to know how you feel about him?"

"There's no point," Allison replied. "Jesse and I don't have a future together. Besides, I've just been a job to him, somebody who was placed in his care for protection. He's never indicated to me that I'm anything else to him."

Shelly released a long, deep sigh. "Men stink. Sometimes I think I'd be better off staying single. I'll be one of those old maids with blue hair and lots of cats."

Allison laughed despite her tears. She couldn't imagine anyone less likely to be an old maid. Shelly was far too vivacious, far too giving to spend her life alone.

"I have a feeling Sam Black won't know what hits him this evening. Within a year you two will be married and expecting a miniature Sam or Shelly."

"From your lips to God's ears!" Shelly exclaimed. "I can't think of anything more wonderful." Shelly sighed once again. "I still think Jesse deserves to know how you feel about him. I mean, maybe he's in love with you but just too shy or afraid to tell you."

"It doesn't matter," Allison said miserably. "Even if he loves me, we could never have a future together."

"I must be missing something here because I don't understand. Why can't you guys be together if you love one another?"

"Shelly, I'm blind. Jesse needs a wife who can be his partner, his helpmate. I'm nothing but a burden to him, and I love him too much to marry him. He'd have to make too many sacrifices with me as a wife."

"But you said your blindness is hysterical. Doesn't that mean it could return at any time? What if you leave here, push Jesse out of your life, then your blindness goes away?''

"What if I stay here, cling to him and the blindness never goes away?'' Allison's words hung in the air, thick and heavy with despair.

Before Shelly could reply, the sound of the front door opening drifted into the kitchen. Allison knew the exact moment Jesse stepped into the kitchen.

She smelled him, the wonderful scent that had come to represent passion and protection, safety and security. She also felt his presence, as if by merely stepping into the room he had filled it with a hot energy.

"Hey, boss," Shelly greeted him as she stood from the table. "Anything new?"

"Not a thing," Jesse replied. He sat in the chair Shelly had vacated, a palpable tension radiating from him. Allison wondered what was going on with him.

"Well, I guess I'll take off," Shelly said. "Allison, think about what we talked about. I'll call you later."

"What was that all about?" Jesse asked when she'd left.

"Oh, nothing. Just girl talk," Allison replied. "What's wrong?" she asked.

"Nothing," he said, but the tension in his voice told her otherwise.

"Jesse, something is wrong. I can hear it in your voice. Has something broken loose on the Casanova case?"

"I wish," he replied. "We're at a dead end. No

leads, no clues to follow, nothing. The worst thing is we need to wait for him to commit his crimes again and hope he'll get sloppy.''

The need to reach out and touch him, grab his hand and offer comfort was enormous, but Allison fought the impulse. After tomorrow she wouldn't be here to offer him anything, not a comforting touch or a warm embrace. In the morning Kent Keller would arrive to take her out of Jesse's life.

''Allison, we need to talk.'' Again Jesse's voice was strained.

Suddenly Allison was filled with tension. ''Okay,'' she said. ''Talk about what?''

''About us.''

Allison's heart seemed to freeze midbeat. ''What about us?''

''Allison, I don't want you to leave tomorrow. Don't go back to Chicago. Stay here.'' The words tumbled from him as if he were afraid that if he didn't say them now as quickly as possible, he might never say them. ''I want you to stay here with me. Share my life with me.''

He took her hand in his. ''Marry me, Allison. Marry me and be my wife.''

Emotion shot through Allison, a complicated blend of pleasure and pain.

For a moment she allowed the sheer joy of his words to seep into her heart. Allison knew nothing in her life would ever be the same again.

Still, a tiny voice niggled at the back of her mind, filling her with doubts, with painful uncertainty.

Did he propose because he needed to make restitution for the guilt he'd suffered about Paul's blindness? Even if they married and her sight eventually returned, she'd never know for sure that it hadn't been the old seeds of guilt that had prompted him to marry her in the first place.

The joy she'd momentarily felt at his words seeped away, unable to sustain beneath the weight of her uncertainty.

"Oh, Jesse," she breathed softly, tears burning hot and thick at her eyes. She pulled her hand from his, not wanting his touch while she shoved him firmly and resolutely out of her life. "I've got a life to return to."

Jesse was silent for a long moment, and Allison's heart constricted as she realized he probably thought she didn't love him, that she'd only used him for convenience...to keep away the loneliness of the nights.

She couldn't leave, couldn't walk away from him and not let him know that he'd captured her heart.

The tears she'd been holding inside spilled outward, trekking down her cheeks in hot, stinging trails. "I can't stay here, Jesse. I can't marry you and be your wife." She swiped at her tears.

"I don't understand." His voice was filled with painful confusion.

"Jesse, I'm blind."

"What does that mean?" he returned unevenly. "I know you're blind. What does that have to do with marrying me?" She heard more than a little hint of frustration in his voice. "Suddenly now you want to embrace the blindness you've refused to discuss or acknowledge since the moment you arrived here?''

Allison frowned. "What's that supposed to mean?"

His chair scooted back and he stood. "Nothing. Never mind."

"No. You brought it up. What are you trying to say to me?"

He paced back and forth in front of where she sat, displacing the air with each pass by her, the floor squeaking softly beneath his footsteps. "It just strikes me as odd that now you are blind, and in all the time we've spent together before this moment, you've refused to believe your blindness has anything to do with your future. What if you stay blind forever?"

Now she sensed an underlying anger in his words. And the anger fed the uncertainty she felt of his love. "If I stay blind forever, then I'll learn how to adjust."

"You certainly haven't started any kind of adjustment while you've been here. You've steadfastly refused to discuss the possibility of being sightless for any length of time."

She wanted to contradict him, suddenly felt the need to be angry, but she knew what he said was right. She had refused to accept the possibility that her blindness might last forever.

"Would you please stand or sit still," she snapped. "It's difficult for me to follow your footsteps when you're pacing so fast." She waited as he once again sat next to her, then drew a deep breath and continued. "You're right," she agreed. "I haven't wanted to admit the possibility that I might spend the rest of my life blind. But now I'm facing the possibility."

"Why can't you face that possibility here...with me?"

The anger she'd sensed in him only moments before was gone, vanished beneath a soft plea that ripped holes through her heart.

"Don't you see, Jesse? If I stay, I'll never know if your proposal was based on real feelings for me or if you're in some way trying to fix what happened in your past. You feel as if you let down Paul. What better way to fix it than to take care of me?"

"Are you finished playing amateur psychologist now?"

She flushed and nodded.

"Maybe the real problem here is your fear of somehow being dependent on anyone. Have you considered the fact that your feelings for me might just be suspect?"

"What are you talking about?" If there was one thing Allison was certain of, it was the love she felt for Jesse.

"Maybe you're a coward, afraid to adjust to your blindness, afraid to deal with what you've been dealt. Maybe if you could see, you wouldn't care about me at all."

"That's ridiculous," she scoffed with a rise of her own anger. "I know what I feel for you, Jesse Wilder." She stood, knowing she needed to escape.

She had to get away before she weakened, before she allowed her selfish need for Jesse to override the knowledge that he was better off without her. "Face it, Jesse. We'll never really know. It's best if we cut our losses and just say goodbye."

She didn't wait for his reply, but instead stumbled from the kitchen and down the hallway, needing the privacy of her bedroom to shed the tears that begged to be released. She needed to cry for what she'd found...and cry for what she'd lost.

She'd only been in the bedroom a brief time when Jesse knocked on the door. "Allison, I've got to leave," he said. "I've put a call in to Shelly to come back here. In the meantime, I'll lock you in."

"I'll be fine," she answered through the closed door, although she knew the words were a lie.

She had a feeling it would take a very long time before she'd feel fine again.

Jesse drove aimlessly down Main Street, trying to sort out exactly what had happened in his kitchen only minutes before.

What had begun as a confession of love and a proposal of marriage had somehow gotten twisted into something complicated and ugly. Where had it all gone wrong?

He tightened his grip on the steering wheel, fighting an overwhelming sense of despair as he thought of a life without Allison in it.

Dammit, he hadn't wanted to fall in love. So far, he'd spent his life just fine alone. But now, alone sounded like hell.

He'd awakened that morning knowing she'd be gone tomorrow, and his heart had ached with the anticipation of her absence. He'd known then he couldn't let her walk away, couldn't let her leave his life without telling her that he loved her. He'd never forgive himself if he didn't at least try for a happily-ever-after with her.

A desolate sigh escaped him. He'd tried…and failed. Allison didn't believe he truly loved her. He tightened his grip once again, anger coursing through him as he thought of her words. How could she believe that somehow he had fallen in love with her in some strange need to heal his past with Paul?

Is it possible that's what your love for her is all about? a tiny voice whispered in the back of his head. He was the first to admit that accident so long ago had scarred him with guilt, dug deep wounds into his soul. But surely that had nothing to do with how he felt about Allison.

He slowed his car as he saw Vic's patrol car approach. He waved his deputy over, then pulled to a stop on the opposite side of the street. He got out of the car and approached Vic's vehicle.

"Hey, Jesse. What's going on?" Vic got out of his car, a worried frown on his face. "Is anything wrong?"

"No, everything is fine. I've got some business out of town to take care of and I'm going to be gone for most of the evening," Jesse explained. "I just wanted to give you a message for Shelly. She should be over at my house by now, staying with

Allison. Could you swing by there and tell her I'll probably be late getting back?''

"Sure. No problem." Vic's curiosity about what business Jesse had out of town was obvious, but Jesse offered no explanation. "I'll swing by your house and let Shelly know the plans."

"Thanks. I appreciate it. I'll check in later." Jesse turned and headed back to his car.

He climbed in behind the steering wheel, but for a long moment didn't start the engine. Someplace in the span of the last few minutes, when he'd seen Vic's car, he'd made the decision.

He'd called Allison a coward for not facing the possibility of a lifetime of blindness, but in truth he was the coward, afraid of facing his own shortcomings, afraid of going back in time and facing his guilt.

Yes, the time had come. It was time to face his past. It was time to go see Paul.

Minutes later he was on the highway heading to Grange City. As he drove, he took in the scenery, consciously memorizing it so he could explain it to Allison. He needed to remember the exact color of the grass, the brilliant hues of the wildflowers he passed.

Then he remembered. After tomorrow he wouldn't be describing things to Allison. He would no longer have the pleasure of being her eyes for her.

He consciously shoved thoughts of Allison aside, needing instead to prepare himself for the meeting with Paul. Perhaps he should have called ahead, made contact by phone. But he was afraid to do that, afraid that Paul would tell him to go to hell. And Jesse wouldn't blame him if he did.

It was an hour drive to Grange City, and once there, a few questions at the gas station on Main Street gained him directions to Paul's house.

It was a pleasant ranch, with late-summer flowers blooming in riotous array along the sidewalk leading to the front door.

Jesse pulled up to the curb and shut off his car, but he didn't get out right away. Instead he sat staring at the house, his thoughts once again filled with Allison.

Had she been right? Did he love her because it somehow eased the pain of him walking away from Paul? He wasn't sure anymore. He'd carried his guilt over Paul for years, letting it fester into a gaping wound. That experience with Paul had colored everything in Jesse's world since that moment in time.

Drawing a deep breath for courage, Jesse opened his car door and stepped out. He had to face this now. He had to make it right, to clear his head where Allison was concerned. This issue, this pain from his past had to be lanced in order to heal.

With long, purposeful strides, he walked to the front door and without giving himself a chance to think, rang the bell.

Somewhere in the back of his mind, Jesse was expecting one of Paul's parents to answer the door. Shock riveted through him when the door opened to reveal Paul.

He wore his blond hair just as he had in high school, the same cowlick he used to curse, sticking up at the crown of his head. He was thinner, and wore dark glasses, but other than that, he looked much the same as he had when he and Jesse had been the best of friends.

"Yes? May I help you?" he asked. His hands touched each side of the door frame, an orienting action Jesse had seen Allison do a dozen times a day.

"Paul." The single word fell from Jesse's lips with a tremble.

Paul tilted his head slightly, his brow above the dark glasses wrinkling. "Jesse?"

"Yeah, it's me."

Paul laughed, the sound tugging Jesse back in time, back to happy, carefree days. "Well, I'll be a son of a gun." He held out a hand. "What in the hell took you so long?"

Jesse grabbed his hand in a hard grip, and in that moment of a simple handshake, his healing began.

Chapter 13

Paul and Jesse had only just sat down inside the kitchen when the front door opened once again. A moment later an attractive blond woman walked in, followed by twin little girls who appeared to be about five years old.

"Daddy! Daddy!" The two munchkins made a beeline to the chair where Paul was seated.

"Ah, if it isn't my little Flopsy and Mopsy," he said as they each tried to crawl up into his lap.

"Here, let me help you." Jesse jumped up to help the woman whose arms were filled with grocery bags.

"Thanks," she said as he took a sack from her and set it on the countertop.

"Honey, the handsome man aiding you right now is Jesse Wilder," Paul said. "Jesse, the gorgeous woman before you is my wife, Ellen."

"Hi, Ellen." Jesse offered her a warm smile, pleased that she returned it with one of her own.

He wondered how much she knew about him, his relationship to Paul and the accident that had stolen Paul's sight. Did she know that Jesse was the one driving that night? That he'd been responsible for the accident?

"And these are Frick and Frack, my two daughters," Paul added, his words causing the twins to giggle a musical chorus.

"We're not Frick and Frack," the one on Paul's left knee explained. "I'm Mindy."

"And I'm Mandy," the twin on Paul's right knee said.

"It's very nice to meet you both," Jesse replied. He could feel the love in the room, the love that radiated between the four people that shared the space of the house. The air positively vibrated with positive energy.

"Jesse, why don't we sit out back and visit while the ladies put away groceries?" Paul suggested.

"Sure."

Jesse followed behind Paul through a back door that led to a screened-in porch. Colorful lounge furniture was complemented by a vast array of green plants, giving the aura of airy cheerfulness.

The two men sat at a resin table in chairs with floral cushions. Before sitting, Paul offered Jesse a soft drink from the compact refrigerator.

Jesse wrapped his fingers around the cold soda can before him. With so many words, thoughts and emotions flooding through him, it was difficult to pick which to speak of first.

"You look good, Paul," he began. "I was expecting your mom or dad to answer the door."

"They retired to Florida six months ago and left me the house," Paul explained.

"You look...happy," Jesse said.

Paul smiled, a trace of young boy in the gesture. "I am happy. There are days I think I might be one of the luckiest people on this earth."

Emotion rose up in the back of Jesse's throat. "I'm glad...I needed to know..." He cleared his throat, trying to regain control of himself, but it was no use.

Years of guilt and betrayal, of sorrow and pain released as Jesse reached for Paul's hand. This man had haunted his dreams for years, cried out Jesse's betrayal from nightmares.

For a moment, Jesse couldn't speak as he fought against the tears that burned like fire at his eyes. "I've thought about you often. I—I'm so sorry, Paul," he finally managed to gasp.

Gently Paul pulled his hand from Jesse's grip. "Sorry? What in the hell are you sorry about? It was an accident, Jesse. A stupid, tragic accident."

"But I should have left the party when you first told me the weather was getting bad," Jesse protested, refusing the easy way out. "It was my fault we were on that road when the ice storm hit. It was my fault we had the accident."

"You crazy dolt," Paul said gently. "Have you been carrying that weight around all these years?

Jeez, Jesse, I could say the same thing, that it was my fault I went through the window of the car. Three times you told me to buckle my seat belt, and three times I ignored you.''

Jesse stared at Paul in startled surprise. He'd forgotten that. He'd forgotten how he'd insisted Paul buckle in and how Paul had told him to quit acting like a mother.

Paul was right. Had he been wearing his seat belt, he probably would have never gone through the windshield. They'd both been foolish kids that night.

However, this information didn't absolve Jesse from his guilt over what had happened after the accident. ''I let you down, man,'' Jesse said. ''I walked away from you because I was afraid I couldn't deal with your blindness.''

''Bull. You walked away from me because my mom was acting like a junkyard guard dog, snapping and snarling at everyone who came near me.'' Paul laughed. ''I know my mother, Jesse, and I certainly wouldn't have crossed her for you.''

''Yeah, but I was relieved when she told me to go away.'' The confession fell from Jesse's lips on a sigh of forlorn pain. This, more than anything had haunted Jesse's very soul, the fact that he'd been relieved not to have to deal with Paul's blindness.

Paul sighed, as well, and raked a hand through his hair, causing his cowlick to become more pronounced. ''And to tell you the honest truth, I was glad you didn't come to see me.''

"I don't blame you," Jesse returned. "You must have been so angry at me."

"At you? Nah. Why would I be mad at you? I didn't want to see you because I was angry at the Fates. I was angry, but more than that I was scared and I sure didn't want my best friend to see me crying and carrying on like a baby."

Paul's cheeks flushed a dull red. "I was a mess for about a month, and I'm glad nobody but my parents saw me like that. It was less a burden to handle it all alone, without having to put on any macho pretense for your benefit."

"I still say I should have been there for you. I wouldn't have cared if you cried," Jesse replied. "I was a coward," he added bitterly.

"You were a kid, like me," Paul countered. "What did we know about how to handle tragedy? Hell, for us, tragedy was a pimple on our chin on Saturday night, or my mom calling me Paulie in front of any girl of any age. We weren't equipped to know how to deal with the real hard stuff."

Paul laughed suddenly. "Speaking of tragedies, remember when Buddy Loreen tried to dye his hair darker?"

"And he came to school the next day with his forehead and ears all black?" Jesse's laughter joined Paul's.

Suddenly they were thrust back in time, sharing stories of boyhood friendship, retying the knots of friendship that had raveled a bit with age, but hadn't broken completely.

Each remembered story, each moment of shared

laughter further healed the pain in Jesse's heart, soothed the guilt away as if it had never existed.

When Ellen invited him to stay for dinner, he readily accepted, not eager to call an end to the magical visit. And it was magic. He and Paul picked up as if it had only been a day since they'd last seen one another.

Throughout dinner, Jesse learned more about Paul's life, that he spent much of his time developing computer programs specifically geared toward the sight impaired.

"Heck, the accident was the best thing that happened to me," Paul said over the evening meal. "It forced me to use my head instead of my brawn. Before the accident, I was certain I was going to be a Hall of Fame football player, so I didn't utilize my brain very much."

"There are days I think he still gets confused about what part of his anatomy he should be using," Ellen said dryly.

After the meal, while the adults were still seated at the table and the twins had gone into their room to play, Jesse found himself telling Paul and Ellen about his work, his life...and about Allison.

"Sounds like the lady has had a tough time," Ellen said when he'd finished recounting the murders that had brought Allison to his care.

"She has, but she's got a lot of heart." A smile curved Jesse's lips as he thought of Allison. "She's funny and bright, beautiful and stubborn."

"Sounds like you're crazy about this Allison," Paul observed.

"I am. I'm in love with her," Jesse answered easily. He drew a deep breath as the realization of what he'd said, what he felt, hit him square in the chest.

Without the guilt, without the self-hate he'd carried for so long, his love for Allison suddenly blossomed vivid and intense inside him.

He realized now she'd been completely wrong. His love for her had nothing to do with unfinished business with Paul. It had everything to do with the woman herself.

"I love her like I've never loved anyone before in my entire life," he exclaimed.

"Didn't you say she was leaving first thing in the morning?" Ellen asked.

"Yeah."

"Then what are you doing sitting here with us?" Paul smiled toward his wife. "He always was slow with the women."

Jesse stood from the table, his need to get back to Mustang and Allison overwhelming. "I hate to eat and run, but you're right. I've got to get back home."

Paul stood and walked him to the front door. Once there, the two men embraced in a warm hug they'd have never allowed in their adolescence. "Don't be a stranger," Paul said. "I've missed you."

"I've missed you, too," Jesse replied warmly.

"And if you really love Allison, don't let her get away."

"Thanks, Paul, for everything. And don't worry,

you haven't seen the last of me. Next time I show up here, hopefully I won't be alone.'' With these final words, Jesse left Paul's house and headed back to his car.

As he left Grange City, the last of the evening sun was sinking down in the sky. When it rose again, Allison intended to walk out of his life.

He stepped on the gas pedal. Not if he could help it. *Somehow, someway,* he had to make her see that they belonged together.

"Shelly, please go," Allison said. "I know it must be getting close to the time you're supposed to meet Sam. Jesse will probably be home soon and I'll be just fine in the meantime."

"You know I can't do that," Shelly protested. "Jesse would kill me if I left you here alone."

Allison frowned irritably. She was tired of requiring a nursemaid, and there was nothing more she wanted than some time alone—time to prepare herself for saying goodbye to Mustang…to Jesse.

"Can't you call Vic and have him come and stay here so you can make your date with Sam?" Allison didn't want to be the reason Shelly couldn't keep her date with her handsome deputy.

"Can't. Vic is on patrol duty this evening."

"Then call him and ask him to check in on me. That should be enough to make Jesse happy, and you can get out of here. Please, Shelly. I just need this evening to be alone."

She felt Shelly's hesitation, knew the young woman was giving her idea credence. "If Vic will drive by occasionally, and I keep the doors and windows locked tight, I'll be fine. I'll make it right with Jesse. I'll tell him I threw you out.''

"All right,'' Shelly relented with a great deal of reluctance in her voice, ''but only if Vic agrees to do frequent drive-by checks.'' As Shelly left the living room and went to the phone in the kitchen, Allison sank back into the sofa cushions with a sigh.

She'd had a headache all afternoon and the evening hours were bringing no relief. She knew it was from all the tears she'd shed into her pillow. Tears for Jesse, tears for herself, tears for the love that should—could—never be. And still the tears pressed dangerously thick behind her eyes.

She was tired of putting on a pleasant air for Shelly, tired of forcing conversation she didn't feel like having. She wanted to be alone. She needed to be alone.

Shelly returned from the kitchen. "Okay, I got hold of Vic and he said he'll drive by here about every fifteen minutes or so until he sees Jesse's car back in the driveway. Are you absolutely sure this is going to be okay?''

"I insist,'' Allison replied, rising from the sofa. Now that Shelly had agreed, she was eager to get the woman out the door and on with her life, hopefully with her Sam.

It seemed only right that at least one of them should get their heart's desire. "Now go. Have fun with Sam and show him that you're the woman he needs in his life.''

Shelly leaned forward and kissed Allison's cheek. "I'm really going to miss you. Would you please try to stay in touch?"

"I will," Allison replied, although it was a lie. There was no way she could stay in touch with Shelly without the pain of Jesse haunting her. Allison knew the only way to survive the heartache was to cut it cleanly and quickly away. She had to cut all ties to Mustang.

"Lock the door behind me," Shelly instructed.

"I will." The moment Shelly stepped outside, Allison closed the door and carefully locked it.

Alone. The silence of the house pressed inward, as empty, as silent as her heart. Had she made a mistake in pushing Jesse away?

Would it be so wrong to just accept his love? Let him decide if he wanted the burden of a blind wife or not? Would it be wrong to be willing to accept his love even if she wasn't sure of the forces that had prompted him to love her?

It was too late. Jesse was gone, and his absence spoke louder than any words he could use. Perhaps he'd needed time to think, and in the time that he'd spent away, he'd realized he didn't want a blind wife and that his love for her had been prompted by his unresolved feelings where Paul was concerned.

In any case, it appeared his plan was to stay gone until he was certain she was already asleep when he returned home. They probably wouldn't have much time together in the morning before Keller arrived to take her back to Chicago.

She should go pack. She'd put it off all afternoon and had refused to think about it this evening. But the evening was waning into night and she knew she wouldn't want to face the packing in the morning.

She started down the hallway, but instead of turning into her bedroom, found herself standing in the center of Jesse's. In this room, his scent remained, and it filled her senses as she grieved what would never be.

Crawling onto his bed, she grabbed his pillow and held it to her chest, the tears once again sliding down her cheeks as deep sobs rent her body.

Maybe this was why her mother had warned her about becoming dependent on a man. Maybe this was why her mother had never sought out love again when her husband had left her. Because it felt like a kind of death when you lost the one you loved.

She didn't know how long she remained on Jesse's bed, crying for the mornings they'd never have together, the nights of passion they'd never share. She only had a sense of time passing, of the evening waning into night.

Wearily she roused herself from the bed and went into her own bedroom. She found her suitcases on the floor of the closet and opened them in the center of the bed.

It didn't take her long to pack the few items she'd brought with her. She lingered over the silk dress Jesse had bought her, unsure if she should take it with her or not. She finally decided to pack it, knowing he wouldn't give it to anyone else and had no use for it.

Besides, she thought, her heart aching, he'd bought it for her because it matched her eyes. When she finished packing, she changed from her clothes and pulled on her nightgown.

For a brief moment, she thought about going back into Jesse's room and crawling into his bed. Just one more night of being held in his arms, feeling his heart beating with her own, tasting his mouth as he drank of hers.

The impulse lasted only a moment. Then she got into her bed and closed her eyes, begging sleep to come quickly and praying that she didn't dream of what might have been.

She didn't know how long she'd been asleep when something awakened her. She remained still as sleep instantly transformed to complete wakefulness.

Jesse must have finally come home, she thought. She turned on her side and once again closed her eyes. Her bedroom door creaked open and still she remained unmoving, assuming Jesse was checking to see if she was asleep.

She didn't want to see him. She didn't want to talk to him. They had nothing left to say to one another, and more talk would only further break her heart.

She tensed as she sensed him coming closer to the bed. The floorboards creaked beneath his weight and he froze for an instant. At that moment she realized it wasn't Jesse in her room. Whoever it was, was bigger than Jesse, and smelled different. Her heart nearly exploded out of her chest.

Before she could respond in any way, large hands slapped tape across her mouth and those same large hands grabbed her forearms in an attempt to still the fight that had come too late.

Her mind reeled. She knew. She knew now who was in her room.

Casanova.

She struggled to get free, kicking her feet, thrashing her body and screaming ineffectually against the barrier of the tape across her mouth.

Somebody help me! Please! Somebody! Jesse…help me! She didn't know if she were screaming the words or if they were only being screamed in her mind.

He released her arms and instead grabbed both her legs and attempted to press her ankles together. She knew what he was doing. He intended to tape her ankles together, then he'd tape her wrists together.

When he had her trussed up, he'd carry her out of the house and drive her to the kissing tree. There he would rape her like he'd done to Maggie. Terror sizzled through her, hot and choking as she thought of being violated.

As he taped her feet, she hit him as hard as she could on the back with her hands. She pulled his hair and tried to scratch at him. He grunted beneath the assault, but held tight to her legs until they were firmly taped together.

As Allison struggled to get free, her mind raced.

He was a big man and he smelled familiar. Too familiar. Recognition fluttered through her. She knew him. She knew his name.

Why? Why was he doing this? What drove him to do such unspeakable acts? She had no time to reflect on these questions. They flitted through her head then were gone, overwhelmed by the instinct for survival, the need to fight.

He tried to grab her hands, but she flailed wildly. She wasn't going to make it easy for him. With one hand, she frantically felt around on her nightstand, seeking something, anything that might be used as a weapon. She heard the bedside lamp fall to the floor and a box of tissues flew aside.

Already she was tiring, her struggles growing weaker. He was going to win. He was bigger…stronger…and she was no worthy opponent.

Her hand closed around something—the soap sculpture—and although it was ineffectual as a weapon, she dropped it next to her. At the same time he managed to grab her arms.

He finished binding her, then picked her up and swung her up over his shoulder like a sack of potatoes. Allison's fear clawed through her, making her want to retch.

Where are you, Jesse? her mind screamed. Please come home now. Please find me before he rapes me.

She knew when he stepped out the front door, felt the cool night air lick at the skin the thin nightgown didn't cover. She renewed her fight, knowing that if he managed to get her in his car, all would be lost.

His beefy hands held her tight against his shoulder and neck, and with her hands and legs bound together, she couldn't manage to break free.

She heard the car door open, then felt herself tossed into the back seat of his vehicle and the car door closed once again. She lay on the seat that smelled of fast-food wrappers and minty soap, trying to catch her breath.

It was hard to breathe against the tape across her mouth. She longed to pull it free and draw deep gulps of air. Instead she focused on the tape that held her wrists tightly together as Casanova got into the front seat and started the engine of the car.

She knew the drive from Jesse's house to the kissing tree took about fifteen minutes. That gave her fifteen minutes to try to get free and form a plan of escape. Otherwise... She steadfastly refused to consider otherwise.

Chapter 14

Jesse drove as fast as he dared, fighting the impulse to use his siren and lights to eat up the miles more quickly. But he hesitated using official equipment for personal business. Besides, fifteen minutes one way or the other won't make that much difference, he told himself.

He felt better than he had in years. He felt clean and whole, eager and open to all possibilities. He hoped having Allison in his life was more than a possibility. He wanted to make her a certainty.

He stepped on the gas pedal, flirting with breaking the speed limit. Allison's name sang through his veins as his heart pumped the rhythm of love.

She'd managed to make him doubt himself, doubt the feelings she evoked in him. But the time spent with Paul had fixed the confusion.

His feelings for Allison had absolutely nothing to do with the tragic accident so long ago and his blind friend. Her blindness was not something he had to fix for his own redemption. He loved her, and it was as simple, and as complicated, as that.

And he'd thought she might love him, too. His heart soared. He couldn't be sure if Allison only believed she loved him because of her current circumstances. It was possible if she ever regained her sight, her love for him would fade.

They'd face that situation if and when it happened. Even if they had six months...a year together, it would be more than worth the risk.

He smiled inwardly at this thought. A year ago, even a month ago, he hadn't been willing to take risks. Risks usually meant loss, and Jesse's heart hadn't been whole enough to gamble on another loss in his life.

But now, the risk of eventually losing Allison was worth taking a chance. He had to take a chance on the hopes that their love was based on nothing more than mutual desire, respect and admiration for one another.

He had to risk his heart to seek his ultimate salvation and future happiness. Somehow, someway, he would make Allison see that his love was a fine, good thing with no hidden agendas involved.

Keller had said he would arrive in Mustang around nine. Jesse glanced at the clock on the dashboard. It was almost 8:00 p.m. and he was only minutes from his home. That gave him thirteen hours to convince Allison to remain in Mustang, to stay with him.

Thirteen hours. He'd never been a superstitious man before and he wasn't about to start worrying now. He simply hoped the number thirteen would prove lucky for him. He couldn't imagine his life without Allison.

He frowned as he pulled into his driveway. His front door stood wide open, spilling light from the living room out into the night.

No other cars were in the driveway and Jesse wondered where Shelly was. And why was the door standing open? He got out of his car, a bad feeling rolling in the pit of his stomach.

Before entering the house, he grabbed his gun and holster. He'd taken it off and locked it in the trunk to go to Paul's, but the apprehension that crept up his spine whispered a warning.

With efficient movements, he strapped on the shoulder holster, then clicked the safety off the gun. With the gun firmly in hand and functioning with an aberrant calm that always arose in him in times of stress, he approached the front door.

Nothing appeared amiss in the living room or kitchen. The house held an unnatural quiet that yelled loudly in Jesse's head. Where was Shelly?

It was possible Allison had sent Shelly away. Allison knew she was no longer in danger from the members of the Renegade Eight. She'd been upset when Jesse had left the house. Yes, it was possible she'd told Shelly to go home, and Allison had gone to bed early to prepare for her trip back to Chicago the next day.

And maybe Shelly hadn't quite gotten the front door closed and the evening breeze had blown it open. His mind worked overtime to provide safe, comforting scenarios, but that didn't ease the trepidation that gripped him as he slowly headed down the hallway.

The hand that held the gun before him was sweaty and his heartbeat pounded harshly, echoing in his head. Surely everything is fine, he told himself. Allison is safe and sound, in bed sleeping.

But as he approached her bedroom, saw the door wide open and the light on, all fantasies of safety fled. He stood in the doorway and stared at the empty room—not just an empty room, but the place of a struggle.

Signs of a fight were evident in the twisted condition of the bedclothes, the lamp that had been knocked to the floor near the bed. Jesse had seen three other bedrooms that looked like this, all victims of Casanova.

His heart seemed to stop beating momentarily. Casanova. Did Casanova have Allison? Before the absolute horror of that thought could seep fully into his brain, he noticed something lying in the center of her bed, something that didn't belong there.

He holstered his gun and stepped closer. The soap sculpture. What was it doing in the middle of her bed? Had Allison placed it there? Had she been trying to tell him something?

Vic.

The name exploded in his head. Was it possible Vic was Casanova? Aware of precious seconds being lost, Jesse threw the soap sculpture back on the bed, turned and raced from the bedroom.

He flew through the living room and out the front door, fumbling his keys out of his pocket as he ran. If Allison was intended to be Casanova's next victim, then he would find her at the kissing tree.

As he backed out of his driveway, he grabbed his radio, then hesitated. Dammit. He couldn't use the radio without Vic being privy to what was being said. He couldn't call for backup. He was definitely on his own.

Vic. Surely not. As Jesse drove toward the kissing tree, his mind tried to comprehend the possibility that his trusted deputy was Casanova.

Maybe the soap had simply fallen on the bed during the struggle. Perhaps it hadn't been a clue left by Allison after all.

But even as he tried to deny the possibility, doubts niggled. Lonely Vic, who had trouble getting dates. Overweight and intensely shy, poor Vic just couldn't find love.

Had his misery over his unpopularity with the opposite sex turned into a seething, malicious hatred of women? A hatred that led to him now raping women? Jesse knew rape was a crime of violence, not sex, a crime bred of enormous rage.

Vic had dated all the victims in high school, and Vic had been rebuffed by all the victims in high school. Jesse squealed around a corner, his mind racing as fast as his car.

Vic was always on patrol when the crimes occurred. He was proficient at picking locks, might have even known where spare keys had been kept for the victim's doors. The women would have trusted him with that information. After all, he was an officer of the law.

Of course, in two of the three cases, it had been obvious that Casanova had entered through an open window. Only at Maggie's had there been no sign of forced entry, no open window to indicate a point of entry. Jesse banged his fist on the steering wheel. How had he been so blind? Or had he chosen blindness because he hadn't wanted to believe. He'd thought he'd known Vic...he didn't want to believe a man he'd called his friend, a man he'd trusted as his deputy, was capable of being Casanova.

Jesse tightened his hands around the steering wheel, agony tightening his chest as he thought of Allison becoming the next victim.

She'd been through so much already. She'd lost her family, lost her sight, but for the most part she'd remained so strong, so courageous. How much more could she handle without a complete break?

He thought of her, bound and gagged, blind and helpless, and a killing rage of his own filled him. The idea that somebody would take by force from her what she'd so willingly given to Jesse, horrified him.

He turned onto the gravel road that would take him to the kissing tree. Gravel banged the bottom of his car, spewed out behind in his wake as he barreled ahead.

He had to get there in time. He had to. And he prayed that Casanova hadn't decided to change his pattern. He prayed Vic hadn't found a new place in town to torment his victims.

Allison's heart beat the rhythm of hope as she realized she'd managed to work one hand free from the tape that had bound them. Her first impulse was to reach up and rip the tape from her mouth and draw deep breaths of air, but she knew that would be a mistake.

He'd instantly see the tape gone from her mouth and know she'd freed her hands. Besides, it was more important she be ready to run, and she couldn't run if her legs remained taped together.

Cautiously she reached down to her ankles, not wanting to alert Vic to what she was doing. Vic had been silent as he drove, and Allison knew he believed his silence was his protection.

As long as the victims couldn't see him, didn't hear his voice, there was no way they would be able to make a positive identification of him. But there was no doubt in Allison's mind that Vic was the man driving the car. Vic was Casanova.

She had just managed to free her ankles when the car pulled to a halt. Vic got out of the car and Allison rolled onto her back, pulling her knees to her chest. He had no idea she was unbound, and she knew she'd have one opportunity to take him by surprise.

She held her breath, praying he opened the door on the passenger side, where she could hopefully manage to give him one good, solid kick in the chest. If he opened the other door, where her head was resting on the seat, there would be no opportunity to kick at him.

Had the other victims tried to fight him? Had they worked themselves free as Vic had driven them to the scene of the intended crime, only to be once again overwhelmed by his superior strength?

Or had the others been too terrified to think, to fight. Not only had they suffered the terror of being taken from their rooms in the middle of the night and bound and gagged, but they'd had the additional terror of sudden blindness. Allison was spared the horror of an unanticipated loss of sight.

She heard the crunch of gravel as Vic walked around the car. She tensed, legs ready to attack. She had no way of knowing when to kick, no way of aiming her offense at any particular portion of his body. She could only depend on dumb luck and hope she scored.

The car door opened and she fought the impulse to instantly kick out. Instead she waited one second…two seconds… Then when she sensed him leaning in to grab her, she slammed her legs outward.

She connected solidly. Vic groaned and she heard him fall backward. Allison shot out of the car like a bullet from a gun. Head down, arms flailing out in front of her, she ran.

There was nothing more terrifying than the act of running in complete and total darkness, not knowing what deadly obstacles may be ahead.

There was nothing more terrifying—unless it was being chased by somebody who was not in complete and total darkness.

She could hear Vic behind her, advancing with sure, steady footsteps. She tore the tape from her mouth, drawing deep gulps of night air, and picked up her pace, praying she didn't smack into a tree and render herself unconscious.

She screamed as the ground suddenly disappeared from beneath her feet and she was falling. Head over heels she tumbled, branches and brush gouging her legs, ripping her gown and scratching her arms and face.

Forever. An eternity of pain. That's what it felt like as she banged against trees, slid across rocks. She finally came to a halt at the base of a tree, her body screaming in pain.

She remained unmoving, trying to still the breaths that came from her in deep, wrenching sobs. Where was Vic? Had he watched her fall? Was he now slowly making his way toward her?

Slapping a hand across her mouth, she held her breath…listening. In the distance she could hear footsteps, but they seemed to have no real purpose or direction. They were tentative…going first one way, then another.

He couldn't see her. The thought filled her with hope. Was it possible the night was cloudy and the woods dense? Was it possible that for this moment in time she and Vic were even in their visual skills?

Wincing in pain, she cautiously moved her legs, then her arms, making sure nothing was broken.

Trying to make as little noise as possible, she moved to the opposite side of the tree and drew herself into a small ball. Hopefully the thick trunk would hide her if Vic came near.

Leaning her forehead against the rough bark of the tree, she listened once again. The footsteps were still distant and still hesitant. He stopped every few steps and she knew he was listening for any sounds that might tell him her hiding place.

Jesse. Allison's heart cried. Would she ever see him again? How silly their little argument seemed at the moment. He'd told her he loved her, wanted to marry her and because of her own pride, and fears, she'd turned him away.

Please let me have another chance, she prayed. She wondered if it would do any good to call out to Vic, let him know she knew who he was. If she talked to him, could she make him stop this insanity? Or would she push him further over the edge? Would she turn a rapist into a killer?

Can he see me? Am I hiding in plain sight? An old childish ditty drifted through her mind. If Vic got close enough, would he be able to see her hair? Her toes?

Vic's footsteps drew nearer and Allison prayed.

As Jesse pulled up toward the kissing tree, his high beams played on the stately old oak.

Nothing.

Nobody.

A wave of despair swept through him.

Had Casanova chosen a new place to commit his

crimes? Dear God, where was Allison? If Vic was Casanova, where would he have taken Allison?

Jesse shut off the engine and got out of his car. He grabbed a high-power flashlight from the back seat, then approached the tree, unsure what he was looking for, but not knowing where else to look.

There was no indication that anyone had been in the area recently. The grass around the base of the tree appeared undisturbed. Yet, even as Jesse stood staring at the trunk of the tree, something niggled in the back of his mind.

The silence.

Jesse had never been to this heavily wooded place and heard such deep, profound silence. No insects chirped, no animals rustled, not a single noise of life resounded. It was an unnatural silence, as if the trees, the nocturnal creatures and the bugs and insects were all holding their breaths.

At the same time Jesse's mind was registering this, his flashlight beam shone on something in the distance. He squinted and took several steps forward.

His heart beat rapidly and his hand tightened around the grip of the flashlight as he realized what he was looking at was the back end of Vic's patrol car.

"Vic!" The name exploded from his lips, filled with rage and tainted by fear.

"Allison." Her name tore from the deepest part of his soul.

He listened, and heard nothing but the frantic beating of his own heart.

He approached the car and shone the light first in the front seat, then in the back. There was nobody inside and nothing looked out of place. But Jesse knew in his gut that Allison had been in the back seat, that she'd been carried from his house and brought here for Vic's insane pleasure.

"Vic!" He yelled again, at the same time drawing his gun. He thought of the big deputy, his right-hand man. Vic had been a friend, a trusted co-worker. Was it possible Jesse was betraying him by believing him capable of being Casanova?

Maybe Vic was out here patrolling and had nothing to do with Allison's disappearance. But even as he sought excuses, he knew deep in his heart that Vic and Casanova were one and the same.

Jesse had studied enough profiles of criminals to know Vic fit the profile for a serial rapist. Why in the hell hadn't he seen it before?

"Vic, dammit, where are you?"

"Jesse? Is that you?" Vic appeared from out of the brush. He looked disheveled and was half out of breath. He shielded his eyes against the glare of Jesse's flashlight. "I'm glad you're here. Something's going on out here."

Jesse holstered his gun and walked toward Vic, fighting the anger that nearly choked him. "Where is she?" he asked, his voice a deadly calm.

"Wha-what are you talking about?" Vic shifted uneasily from one foot to the other. "I was driving patrol by here and saw a car take off in a hurry. At the same time I saw somebody run off in the woods. I've been investigating."

"I'm going to ask you again, Vic. Where is Allison?"

Jesse fought the impulse to wrap his hands around Vic's neck, squeeze until his eyes bulged and Vic was shouting what Jesse wanted to know.

"Gosh, Jesse. How would I know where Allison is?"

"If you've touched her, I'll kill you. If you've harmed a hair on her head, I'll see you in hell." Jesse's voice trembled with the force of his emotion.

Vic blanched. "I don't know what you're talking about," he said stubbornly.

They both turned at the rustling sound of somebody approaching. Allison broke into the clearing. Her cheeks were bloody, her nightgown torn and she was limping. Her hands were out before her, as if to ward off a blow.

"Jesse?" she whispered.

He rushed to her. "I'm here," he said, enfolding her into his embrace. "It's all right. You're safe now." She sobbed into his shirtfront. Words jumbled in with the sobs, incoherent half sentences that spoke of her terror.

"Oh my gosh," Vic said. "Allison, what happened?" He took a step toward them, but once again Jesse drew his gun. This time he pointed it at Vic's chest.

"Stay right where you are, Vic, until I sort this all out," Jesse said.

"Jesse, you can't believe I had anything to do

with this?'' Vic stared at Jesse with haunted eyes. ''I just stumbled on all this by accident.''

''Vic is Casanova.'' They were the first real clear words Allison spoke.

''That's crazy,'' Vic replied, his voice a mere whisper. ''Allison, you don't know what you're saying.''

''Are you certain?'' Jesse asked Allison.

She stepped out of Jesse's embrace and drew a deep breath, as if seeking the very last modicum of courage she possessed. ''Vic, you came into my bedroom and you taped my wrists and ankles. You taped my mouth so I couldn't scream for help, then you picked me up out of my bed and carried me to your car.''

''No,'' Vic whispered in protest.

''I knew it was you the moment you entered the room,'' she continued. ''I smelled your scent, I knew your touch. It was you, Vic.''

Vic opened his mouth as if to protest yet again, then he appeared to crumble into himself. ''It was the legend,'' he said, tears springing to his eyes.

''Throw down your gun, Vic,'' Jesse said.

''But I need to make you understand,'' Vic exclaimed.

''Throw down your gun and then we'll talk.'' Jesse watched as Vic carefully removed his gun and threw it into the grass nearby. ''Vic, I'm going to have to handcuff you.''

''I understand,'' Vic replied, his voice once again just above a whisper.

Jesse touched Allison on the shoulder. ''Just

stand tight. I'll be right back by your side in a minute." He walked over to Vic and handcuffed the deputy, then instructed him to sit on the ground.

"Jesse, I just want to explain...."

"I'm going to put in a call for Shelly and Sam to meet us here, then you can talk all you want," Jesse said.

"Can't you call somebody else?" Allison asked. "Shelly and Sam are on their first date tonight."

For a moment, Jesse couldn't speak. So great was his love for her. There she stood, bloodied and ragged, having suffered who knew what, but her first thought was for a young couple enjoying their first date.

"I don't think they'll mind the interruption," he replied. He made the call, then returned to where Allison had sank down to the ground. "Are you okay?" he asked softly, his gaze on Vic, who sat with his head hanging down.

She nodded. "He didn't... I got away. I ran...then I fell—" She broke off, as if too exhausted to say more.

"I wouldn't have hurt her," Vic said. He raised his head and looked at Jesse. "You've got to believe me. I wouldn't have hurt her at all. I just wanted to make the legend come true. That's all I ever wanted. I only kissed them beneath the tree, that's all."

"What about Maggie?" Jesse asked.

"I didn't have anything to do with what happened to Maggie," Vic protested vehemently. "I never would do that to a woman. Somebody else hurt Maggie, somebody who wanted everyone to believe it was Casanova. I only kissed them, Jesse, that's all I did.''

For some reason, Jesse believed him. Sadness swept through him. How had a charming legend become so twisted in Vic's mind? "Did you really believe if you kissed a girl beneath the tree, she'd love you forever?" Jesse asked Vic softly.

Vic shrugged. "Nothing else was working. They say legends sometimes have their basis in fact. I hoped—" He broke off and hung his head forward once again.

At that moment, the sounds of a siren could be heard in the distance. Jesse helped Allison to her feet. When Sam and Shelly pulled up, Jesse instructed Shelly to immediately take Allison to the hospital. "And tell them to keep her there until I get there," he said.

"What are you going to do?" Allison asked.

"Sam and I are going to take Vic in, then we're going to arrest a rapist," Jesse replied.

Chapter 15

"Really, I'm fine," Allison said for the hundredth time in the last hour. She sat in the hospital waiting room. Next to her sat Shelly, who alternately squeezed her hand and sobbed. "Bumps and bruises—that's all the doctor found."

"I just can't believe I left you alone and this all happened." Shelly burst into a renewed crying jag.

"You couldn't know that the man who was supposed to help protect me was the one I had to fear," Allison replied. "Besides, it all worked out just fine. Jesse caught Casanova and I'm no worse for the wear."

She pulled the thin, hospital-issue robe more firmly around her, trying not to remember the moments of terror she'd suffered at Vic's hands.

"I just can't believe it was Vic all along." Shelly

blew her nose. "I should have seen it. He was obsessed with making the case that Maggie's assailant was a copycat, not Casanova. One of us should have suspected something."

"Let it go, Shelly," Allison said wearily. "It's over now." Allison ached in every part of her body, but what ached the deepest, the most profoundly, was her heart. She needed Jesse. She needed to tell him that she'd been a fool to turn her back on what he'd offered her.

Was it too late? Had he changed his mind? The thought of spending the rest of her life without him was almost as terrifying as the ordeal she'd just gone through.

"Poor Vic," she said suddenly. "He must have been desperate for love."

"Yeah, it is kind of sad, isn't it?" Shelly agreed soberly. "He must have been so lonely, so hopeless, he was willing to try a stupid legend to see if it would work. He would have had better luck going to a gypsy and buying a love potion."

Allison considered her feelings for Jesse. Was she desperate? She wanted to build a life with him, wanted to share dreams with him. She wanted mornings and nights of him lying next to her in bed. Was she desperate? No.

If Jesse didn't truly love her as she did him, she'd survive. Her heart would hurt, and it might take her a long time before she gambled on love again, but one thing was certain. She would never go back to being the woman she'd been before.

Before John's and Alicia's deaths, before her

time in Mustang, Allison had consciously avoided relationships, afraid of being too dependent, afraid of giving away pieces of herself.

Mustang, and Jesse, had opened her heart to possibilities. She would never again close herself off to love.

"What time is it?" she asked.

"Almost midnight," Shelly replied. "And here comes Jesse." She stood and Allison did the same. "Hi, boss. Who did you arrest for Maggie's rape?"

"First things first," Jesse said. He stepped in front of Allison and cupped her hand in his palms. "Are you okay? What did the doctor say?"

"He said bed rest and aspirin. I'm just scratched and dented a bit, but fine." She wanted to lean against him, let him wrap her in his arms and hold her close. But all too quickly he withdrew his hands from her and she sank back into the chair.

"So, who did you arrest?" Shelly asked eagerly.

"Burt Landry," Jesse replied.

"You're kidding." Both Shelly and Allison gasped in surprise.

"He raped her, then he became her comfort, her protector." Jesse's voice was laced with disgust. "When Maggie broke up with him, Burt wasn't a happy camper. The Casanova incidences gave him the idea."

"A truly sick idea," Allison said.

"Yeah. Anyway," Jesse continued, "he raped her, then ran to comfort her, and in her fear and confusion she readily took him back into her life."

"Did he confess?" Shelly asked.

"Only after Sam and I hinted we had a witness." Jesse sighed. "As we took him away, he was begging Maggie to forgive him, telling her he'd only done it because he loved her." Jesse wrapped an arm around Allison's shoulders. "Come on, let's get you home. It's been an incredibly long night."

They said goodbye to Shelly, who left with Sam, then Jesse and Allison got into his car and headed toward home.

"Jesse, would you do me a favor?" she asked.

"Just name it."

"Take me back to the kissing tree."

"Why?" he asked in surprise.

"I just need to go back there." She sensed his hesitation. "Please, Jesse, for me."

"Okay," he agreed.

They drove for a few minutes in silence. "I guess the crime wave in Mustang is over," she finally said.

"Thanks to you."

She laughed, then winced as her bruised ribs rebelled. "I didn't do anything but become a near victim."

"That's not true," he protested. "You positively identified Vic as the person who took you from the bedroom. If you hadn't been so certain, Vic might not have confessed and things would have been much more complicated than they were."

"It was his soap," she said. "Vic always smelled like minty soap, just like the little sculptures he made. When he got close to me, I knew it was him." She shivered, remembering her horror. "What I didn't know was if he'd rape me or not."

"You are the most brave woman I've ever known," Jesse said softly. "It took a lot of guts to run from him, especially not being able to see."

She smiled. "At the moment it happened, the alternative was less attractive than knocking myself out by running into a tree." She shifted positions. "The best thing that happened was me falling. I tumbled and rolled away from Vic and he couldn't find me.

"And I thought I'd never get to you. I could hear your voice, knew you were there. Thank goodness you have a voice that carries."

The car came to a halt. "We're at the tree," Jesse said.

"I want to get out." Allison reached for her door handle.

"Wait," Jesse instructed. "I'll come around for you. I don't want you to tumble and roll any more tonight."

She waited while he shut off the engine, then got out of the car and came around to her door. She knew what she intended to do, but she couldn't guess what the results would be.

"Here we go," he said as he opened her car door and helped her out.

"Take me to the tree. I want to stand next to it."

"Okay," he said, but she could hear the bewilderment in his voice.

He took her by the arm and led her several steps. "Allison, what's going on?"

"Are we beneath the kissing tree?" she asked. Nerves rattled inside her, and her palms suddenly felt damp with sweat. What if it was too late? What if he'd changed his mind?

"We're directly beneath the branches, right next to the trunk."

Allison reached one hand out, her fingers making contact with the rough bark. "Describe the tree to me, Jesse."

"It's a big oak tree."

She smiled and reached a hand up to touch his cheek. "You can do better than that."

He captured her hand in his and drew it to his chest. "It's a huge tree, with twisted branches that give it character. The leaves are big, forming a large canopy, and they're just starting to change colors with the approach of fall."

"It's a beautiful tree," she said softly.

"Yeah, it is. Although tonight it seems sort of tainted by everything." Jesse sighed and she could feel his heartbeat against her palm. "This was supposed to be a place of young love and romance. The legend was supposed to inspire hope and the promise of love forever."

"We can't let it remain something tainted and ugly," she said softly.

"How can we change it?" he asked.

"We can make the legend come true." She felt his heartbeat quicken, as did her own.

"The legend is about forever," he said. "You kiss a girl beneath the kissing tree and her heart belongs to you forever. What happens if you regain your sight?''

"I might not." It was the first time she'd admitted the possibility of a lifetime of darkness. "It's possible I could be blind forever. Could you handle that?"

"Absolutely. In fact, I have an old friend, whose acquaintance I renewed this afternoon. He might be willing to teach you Braille, or anything else you might need to learn to cope."

"You saw Paul." She smiled, pleased that he'd found the courage to face his past.

"And seeing Paul made me realize just how much I love you. Allison, my love for you is about you, not about Paul. I want to build a life with you."

"I don't want to be a burden," she confessed painfully.

"My love, the only burden in my life would be if you weren't in my life. I love you, Allison."

"And I love you," she replied, tears of happiness stinging her eyes.

"I want to marry you. I want to live my life with you. I want to—"

"Shut up and kiss me, you fool!" she exclaimed.

His mouth captured hers in a fiery kiss that sent tingles of pleasure up and down her spine. And in the midst of the kiss, she felt the magic of the legend, knew their love would be the forever kind.

Despite the fact that she was blind, she could see all that she needed to see, all that was important. She could see Jesse's love in his kiss, feel his love in the beating of his heart, knew his love as it wrapped around her.

When the kiss finally ended, Jesse picked her up in his arms. "Come on, let's go home."

Home. Yes. She snuggled against him. Home with Jesse. Forever.

Epilogue

Jesse stood next to the preacher and waited impatiently for his bride-to-be to appear. It had been three months since Vic's and Burt's arrests, three months since Jesse and Allison had shared the magical kiss beneath the kissing tree.

Now he stood in the community center, with what seemed to be the entire town of Mustang crowded into the folding chairs, waiting for the wedding that would transform him from the elusive bachelor to contented married man.

Millicent Creighton sat in the front row, her face wreathed in a smile that indicated she thought herself personally responsible for the happy occasion.

She has a wedding cake on her head, Jesse realized in astonishment. Her infamous hat sported a three-tier white cake complete with two tiny figurines at the very top. God bless the quirky people of Mustang, he thought.

Ellen also sat in the front row. At least once a week Jesse and Allison got together with the couple for an evening. The four of them had become good friends, and Paul was helping Allison learn the finer points of being blind.

Jesse straightened as Mindy and Mandy appeared at the end of the aisle. Clad in pale pink dresses, they walked slowly and threw rose petals along the aisle. Immediately behind them was Shelly, who looked radiant as she walked with Sam down the aisle.

And there she was. Allison. His heart. His life. She wore a long, traditional gown of lace, and a veil covered her features. His heart expanded with love as he watched Allison, escorted by Paul, slowly walk down the aisle.

Two people who had made a profound difference in his life. How lucky he was to have them both. As Paul gave him Allison's hand and Ellen led her husband to his seat, Jesse raised the veil and looked into the face of the woman he loved.

She was radiant, positively glowing. "Thank you for being my eyes," she said softly.

"Thank you for teaching me how to see," he replied.

The preacher cleared his throat. "Shall we begin?"

Jesse smiled, as did Allison, and he knew she was thinking the same thing he was. They had already begun. This ceremony was really just a formality. They had pledged their love three months before, beneath the branches of the kissing tree. They were bound—intrinsically, forever—through legend and love.

Allison awoke slowly, smiling even before full consciousness claimed her. Jesse was wrapped around her, his body snuggly warm against hers. They had been married a month, and still she awakened each morning thrilled to find herself in his arms.

She opened her eyes and brightness exploded. She instantly closed them again. Her heartbeat raced. Had she imagined it? She was afraid to try again, afraid not to.

Drawing a deep breath, she opened her eyes once again. Fuzzy…bright…but slowly the fuzz shifted and shapes began to form.

Tears of happiness blurred her new vision, and she reached a hand up to quickly swipe them away. Jesse. She turned her head to get her first view of the man she loved.

He slept on his side, his face mere inches from hers. A beautiful, beloved face. He looked just as he had in her mind. His dark hair was slightly unruly. His eyebrows were thick, his lashes long and full. His nose was straight with the tiniest bump on the bridge. And his lips were soft and sensual in shape. She'd married a hunk.

She'd have loved him if he'd had three eyes and a horn in the center of his forehead. For it was his heart, his soul that had connected with hers. Still, it was nice to know she would never tire of looking at him. Looking at him!

She sat straight up and groaned.

"What—what's the matter?" Jesse asked.

"Nothing," she replied.

"Then come back here where you belong," he murmured, his arm tugging her back against his body.

"I can't."

"Can't what?"

"I don't think I can ever sleep in this bedroom again," she said.

Jesse opened his eyes, rolled over on his back and raked a hand through his hair. "What are you talking about?"

"This is the ugliest wallpaper I've ever seen in my life," she said.

"I warned you it was bad." Jesse sat up. "The ugliest you've ever seen?" he said, his voice a whispered question. "Allison?"

She turned and looked at him. "Yes, it's so ugly." Tears once again blurred her vision. "It's beautiful. You're beautiful." She jumped up on her knees and cupped his face with her hands. "Jesse Wilder, you are the most gorgeous man I've ever seen in my life."

"You can see me?"

She laughed deliriously. "Every whisker, you handsome man."

He grabbed her to him and she sensed a kind of desperation in his embrace. "I'm so glad for you," he murmured into her hair.

"Jesse." She broke the embrace and once again touched his face. She saw the joy in his eyes, saw the joy mixed with something else. "My love, I can see you're happy for me. And I can see that you're worried.''

"I am happy for you," he agreed, his forehead wrinkling a bit. "But things will be different now." He laughed with a touch of uneasiness. "Change is always a little worrisome."

"Ah, Jesse, even if I were blind, I'd be able to see what's bothering you." She snuggled against him. "I'm not running back to Chicago. I love you and this is where I belong. If I'm blind I want to be here, and if I'm not blind, this is where I want to be. Besides—" she focused her attention once again on the wallpaper "—I figure if everyone in Mustang has as bad a taste in decorating as you do, my new business as an interior decorator should boom."

He laughed and she drank in the vision of his laughter. "Do you have any idea how much I love you?" he asked.

"Show me," she said huskily, then grinned. "And keep in mind, I can see every move you make."

And he did. And she did.

* * * * *

In December 2000, look for
STRANGERS WHEN WE MARRIED
by Carla Cassidy—Book 6 in
A YEAR OF LOVING DANGEROUSLY,
the exciting, action-packed 12-book
continuity series from Intimate Moments.

ATTENTION,
LINDSAY McKENNA FANS!

**Morgan Trayhern has three brand-new missions
in Lindsay McKenna's latest series:**

**Morgan's men are made for battle—
but are they ready for love?**

The excitement begins in July 2000, with
Lindsay McKenna's 50th book!

MAN OF PASSION
(Silhouette Special Edition® #1334)
Featuring rugged Rafe Antonio, aristocrat by birth,
loner by choice. But not for long....

Coming in November 2000:

A MAN ALONE
(Silhouette Special Edition® #1357)
Featuring Thane Hamilton, a wounded war hero on his way
home to the woman who has always secretly loved him....

*Look for the third book in the series in early 2001! In the
meantime, don't miss Lindsay McKenna's brand-new,
longer-length single title, available in August 2000:*

MORGAN'S MERCENARIES:
HEART OF THE WARRIOR

Only from Lindsay McKenna and
Silhouette Books!

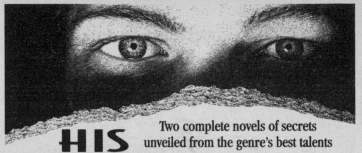

Silhouette invites you to come back to Whitehorn, Montana...

MONTANA MAVERICKS

WED IN WHITEHORN—
12 BRAND-NEW stories that capture living and loving beneath the Big Sky where legends live on and love lasts forever!

M·M

June 2000—
Lisa Jackson *Lone Stallion's Lady* (#1)

July 2000—
Laurie Paige *Cheyenne Bride* (#2)

August 2000—
Jennifer Greene *You Belong to Me* (#3)

September 2000—
Victoria Pade *The Marriage Bargain* (#4)

And the adventure continues...

Available at your favorite retail outlet.

Silhouette®
Where love comes alive™

Look Who's Celebrating Our 20ᵗʰ Anniversary:

Celebrate **20** YEARS

"In 1980, Silhouette gave a home to my first book and became my family. Happy 20ᵗʰ Anniversary! And may we celebrate twenty more."

—*New York Times* bestselling author
Nora Roberts

"Twenty years of Silhouette! I can hardly believe it. Looking back on it, I find that my life and my books for Silhouette were inextricably intertwined.... Every Silhouette I wrote was a piece of my life. So, thank you, Silhouette, and may you have many more anniversaries."

—International bestselling author
Candace Camp

"Twenty years publishing fiction by women, for women, and about women is something to celebrate! I am honored to be a part of Silhouette's proud tradition— one that I have no doubt will continue being cherished by women the world over for a long, long time to come."

—International bestselling author
Maggie Shayne

INTIMATE MOMENTS®
Silhouette®